WINTER HAWK

RACHEL GRANT

JANUS
PUBLISHING

Fiona Carver

Dangerous Ground

Crash Site

Flashpoint

Tinderbox

Catalyst

Firestorm

Inferno

Romantic Mystery

Grave Danger

Paranormal Romance

Midnight Sun

Writing as R.S. Grant

The Buried Hours

*This one is for Serena Bell,
I can't imagine where I'd be without our plotting sessions and
monthly cocktails and tapas night. Thank you for becoming
an integral part of my writing world and for letting me be
part of yours.*

Chapter One

Virginia
December

Nate Sifuentes wished he'd silenced his cell phone before crawling into bed at three a.m., but he'd had no reason to expect an early call the morning after Raptor's official company holiday party. Everyone knew that even normal Sundays were for sleeping in.

But this wasn't a normal Sunday. For the first time in company history, the corporate office was closing down for a full two weeks to celebrate Hanukkah, Christmas, Kwanzaa, and the New Year. As Nate didn't have any ongoing security clients at the moment, the closure meant he couldn't be called in on new jobs, giving him an unscheduled two-week vacation.

Whoever was calling just before eight a.m. this

morning needed to be shot. With a pellet gun, because he wasn't a monster. But still. Shot. At short range. At least a dozen times.

He checked caller ID and changed his mind. Two dozen times. And forget the basic pellets. Paintballs. At least one hit to unprotected junk.

Seriously, after forty-one years, his older brother knew better than to call this early on a Sunday.

The phone went blessedly silent, only to resume ringing a minute later. Freddy had a death wish. Nate picked up the phone. "Someone better be dead or in the hospital."

"Think of how shitty you'd feel if that were really the case," Freddy said, his voice far too cheerful for the early hour.

"Fine. Tell me what you want and I'll decide if hospitalizing you is warranted."

"Stop being so dramatic, baby bro. I just need a favor."

"My first staycation when I'm not stranded in Alaska in six years, and you wake me at eight to ask a favor? It better be a kidney you need, man, or you'll regret this. Like, worse than you regret your mullet years."

"That's the worst you can come up with? My ultracool, retro-nineties mullet?"

"I was up until three. I'm not exactly bringing my A game to this, but for the record, you should regret the mullet. There is no decade in which they were ever cool."

"Listen, one of my regular clients called this morning with an urgent job. Because it's the weekend before the holidays, none of my regular drivers can take it, and I promised Angelica and the kids we'd do Christmas in the city today—see the National Christmas Tree, the works—or I'd do it myself. But it's big bucks. Like…Christmas bonus big. For two hours work, tops. I know you could use a bonus."

That got Nate's attention. Freddy owned a car service that catered to the powerful and wealthy who worked in or visited the nation's capital, and his big brother was right, Nate *could* use a bonus. He did okay with Raptor, but he was an oddity among employees, one of the few hires from Robert Beck's era, before Alec Ravissant bought the company. As a result, he'd never been quite trusted by Rav, CEO Keith Hatcher, or anyone in the DC home office.

Six months ago, Nate had transferred to Virginia so he could be near Freddy and his family. Now that he was situated at the heart of the company, the disparity was obvious, and he was fed up. He had more seniority and experience than Sean Logan, but Sean was the golden boy, one of Rav's very first hires, while Nate, who'd been in the military—and Special Forces—and with Raptor longer, lingered at the trainer and occasional operative level while Sean dabbled in management and got to cherry-pick his assignments. As of a week ago, the guy was officially engaged to Rav's cousin.

Might as well make him heir apparent.

Yet, Nate had no beef with Sean. He liked the guy and would trust him to have his back to the end of time. But it still rankled that he was waking up to a holiday bonus offer, and it wasn't coming from the company he'd given the last eight years of his life to.

"Dude. I'm on vacation."

"Please, man. Seriously, it will be two hours tops. Probably only thirty minutes. A quick assignment. Given that it's the Sunday before Hanukkah and Christmas and this is a special case—a person is getting fired and they need a ride home—the base rate is a grand. You pocket seven fifty, ExecRides gets the rest. You can't tell me Raptor pays that good."

Freddy had a point. Raptor paid him well, but not seven-hundred-and-fifty-for-two-hours well. There had to be a catch. He rubbed his hand over his face in an attempt to wipe the sleep away. Too much wine and too little sleep made for a fuzzy brain.

"You charge a grand for a two-hour job? What kind of car service are you running, bro?"

"This is a high-security job. The pickup is at a military base."

"Which base?"

"Washington Navy Yard."

"It must be a contractor getting fired," he said. It was the only scenario that made sense, given that military personnel didn't get fired, they were discharged, and it didn't happen on a dime.

"Yeah. They'll be escorted to the gate by security. My job is to have someone on the other side to take them home. It's standard procedure for government and private sector firings in touchy circumstances."

"You do a lot of these kinds of firing pickups?" Nate asked.

"Two or three a month. Usually these jobs are short and sweet and bill out for a few hundred. More than we get for the average grocery run. But because this one is happening on the Sunday before Christmas, I asked for more and got it."

"Why do you think they agreed?"

"My guess is the employee is being blindsided and will cry or curse for the entire drive. The client wants this done neat and clean and over with."

"Sounds like a party."

"It will definitely suck."

"Being canned before the holidays can also make a person very vocal with company secrets. Your client could be hoping to buy your loyalty."

"Oh, that's part of it for sure. They're probably worried word will get out the company is being fired by the military. The guy stressed several times what a good customer they've been and if this is handled well, there will be more high-end jobs in the future."

"Who's the client?"

"Hathaway-Hollis. Better known as HH."

"The drone manufacturer? They're making military-grade goods now?"

"Yes, word is the military requested a prototype after seeing what the toy models could do."

Nate drummed his fingers on his leg. Since before Thanksgiving, he'd been seeing news reports saying the metallic silver drones with the bright red HH logo were the must-have toy this holiday season. With Christmas and Hanukkah happening in the same week this year, the skies were about to be flooded with the irritating things.

It appeared at the same time HH was seeing record-breaking sales, they'd screwed up a government contract. No wonder they wanted this handled discreetly.

He closed his eyes, but sleep no longer beckoned. He'd be lying if he claimed he wasn't intrigued. The Navy Yard was just thirty minutes from the Raptor compound, so at most he'd lose three hours of his life. "Wait. Can I drive my Raptor SUV? I'd lose an hour each way if I have to pick up one of your vehicles." Freddy's business was based in Maryland, on the opposite side of DC from the Virginia compound where Nate lived and worked.

"If it's cool with your boss that you use a Raptor vehicle, I don't care. But ExecRides still gets a quarter cut."

"I'll clear it with Keith."

"So you'll do it?"

Nate sighed. There was never really a chance he'd say no. And hell, he'd give ExecRides his share because Freddy and his family were the only people he bought Christmas presents for anyway. He could put up with an angry or crying employee for an hour or two if it meant a grand for Freddy. He imagined Mikaela and Max waking up on Christmas morning to see new bicycles waiting for them and said, "Yes. I'll do it."

*L*eah Ellis glanced at the clock, then rolled her shoulders and cracked her neck. She'd been sitting hunched over too long. But she was so close to finishing this module. She had an hour before she needed to leave for the tour.

She felt positively wild taking a few hours off for herself this afternoon and evening. Her New Year's resolution would be to find work-life balance, but she had ten days before she needed to worry about that and far too much work to complete in such a short period of time.

She'd be further along on the government contract, except for the last week she'd had to clock out at six so she could go home and work on fixing the code for the holiday drones.

She hadn't gotten more than five consecutive

hours of sleep in days because that idiot Dex had screwed up the firmware update. Now, she'd had to fix it while still being expected to hit the government contract milestones.

The job should have gone to Kevin if it was too much for Dex, and anger stirred every time she remembered the words in Dex's email explaining why the task should fall on her: *You don't celebrate Christmas and don't have family. You don't need time off now like the rest of us.*

She'd stuffed the resentment and done the work, not for the reasons he gave but because Peacemaker was her baby and she couldn't let Dex—or Kevin—screw it up. She'd finished at two a.m. this morning and now could give all her attention to the military.

She'd come in today to put in a few hours and get caught up. She'd missed Friday's deadline, but she'd have the beta test ready by tomorrow afternoon. Given that nearly everyone in the Navy Yard offices had opted to take Christmas week off—one of the benefits of government use-or-lose vacation time that she didn't get to enjoy as a contractor—her slight delay was a nonissue. Captain Sullivan had waved her off when she'd explained the problem on Friday, saying his in-laws had arrived in town the day before and he wouldn't be able to review the beta test until after Christmas anyway.

With that assurance, she was being downright reckless and going forward with her plan to take a few hours off to enjoy the candlelight tour of Mt.

Vernon. It was fitting that she'd see George Washington's home by candlelight on the first night of Hanukkah. Her mother would have loved that.

She stared at the computer screen. She was so damn tired. Maybe she should cut out now. What good would another hour do? She had days to finish setting up the beta test.

Instead of quitting, she pulled out her sketchpad and ink pen. The drawing was abstract, boxes and lines, but it organized her thoughts, helped her focus on what remained to be done in the system design. Almost without realizing it, she set the notepad aside and her fingers were back on the keyboard, moving variables around, connecting lines of code in new ways.

She worked alone, but her office had windows on three sides. It was a security measure necessary for the type of work she did at the Navy Yard and had taken some getting used to in the last three weeks, but on days like today—when only workaholics or coders close to a breakthrough were working—she didn't feel like a fish in a bowl. There was no one in the outer offices. The only people in the extremely secure building were likely the marines who provided security at the front door, so it surprised her when movement on the security monitor that faced her desk caught her eye. Two marines approached the outer office.

The monitor had been another security feature to get used to. It showed the office exterior in case armed gunmen stormed the building and she needed to shut the system down before they found a way to hijack military drones.

The pair moved closer, and Leah saw the letters "MP" on an armband. These weren't just marines; they were military police. They crossed the room with purpose, faces blank. All at once, she knew why they were there, and a cold chill ran down her spine.

Captain Sullivan had been fine with her missing the deadline, but others in the chain of command weren't so forgiving.

Her belly clenched. She had mere seconds to decide what to do. Her fingers flew across the keyboard. She needed to delete the beta test. Incomplete as it was, it could be compromised. But if she was wrong about why the MPs were here, she'd be fired for destroying her work.

So instead she buried three weeks of work in the system and generated a code for the file path, then yanked open her desk drawer looking for something, anything, she'd be allowed to remove from this room.

Nothing in the desk. There was no way she'd be allowed to keep the sketchpad, plus it was bound. All at once, it hit her. The printout of her ticket to the candlelight tour. She grabbed it from her coat pocket and smoothed it out, then put it in the manual feed tray and hit Print.

The outer door opened, but the printer was

beneath her desk, not visible to the MPs—a Black woman and an Asian man—as they crossed the room.

She pulled the ticket from the output tray and slipped it into a desk drawer.

The MPs reached her office door and her hands were back on the keyboard, erasing code and killing the beta test.

The door opened. "Remove your hands from the keyboard, ma'am," the Asian MP said.

"I can't leave my files open. It would violate all security protocols." She kept typing.

"Step away from the computer," the woman said. She placed her hand on her weapon but didn't draw. Leah appreciated that consideration.

A glance at the screen showed the files disappearing. She raised her hands and stood, facing the two MPs. "So, what's going on?"

The man gave a faint smile. "I'm pretty sure you've guessed."

She shrugged. "Until I get official word from my supervisor, my guesses mean nothing."

"You have five minutes to collect your personal belongings," the woman said.

The phone on the desk rang.

"You may answer that," the man said.

Government phones didn't have caller ID, but she didn't need to see the name on a screen to know it must be one of her bosses at Hathaway-Hollis.

They'd have been told what was happening before the MPs were called.

She picked up the handset. "What's up, Tim?" she said in a cheerful voice.

"Uh…um…" The man stumbled, clearly caught off guard by her casual greeting. He cleared his throat. "We've been informed by your supervisor at the Washington Navy Yard that your services are no longer appreciated. You are terminated immediately and are to hand over your Navy ID, your company-provided cell phone, and the keys to the townhouse."

Fear shot through her. They weren't messing around. "You can't lock me out of my home."

"As the townhouse is provided by Hathaway-Hollis and is not in your name, you know we can. Given the nature of your work for the military, the NSA is sealing the townhouse. It must be searched before you're allowed reentry to collect your belongings. With the holidays, this will likely take several days. I'm sure you understand why this is necessary."

She knew this kind of lockout was, in fact, a stipulation of her living arrangement. Her work on getting the HH drone technology integrated into the US military system meant she had direct, unfettered access to highly classified and encoded servers. If someone hacked a military drone, she'd be among the first suspects.

"In addition," Tim said, "you are to turn over

your company credit card and the key to your company car."

"Wait, am I being fired from this contract *and* HH?" She was the brains behind the big product launch that had Hathaway-Hollis drones on every kid's wish list, and Tim Hathaway knew it.

"You're being suspended without pay as HH conducts our own investigation, but I think it's safe to say your tenure with Hathaway-Hollis is over."

"This is bullshit. If this is about missing the beta test deadline, you know it's because I had to fix Peacemaker." Terminating her like this for failing to reach a deadline was extreme, especially considering Captain Sullivan had given her a pass.

"The military doesn't have to provide cause for termination of contractors."

"No. But HH does."

"Which is why there will be an investigation."

At the same time Tim spoke, the female MP held out her hand and said, "ID and CAC card."

Leah pulled the lanyard with her Navy Yard ID from her neck and pulled her Common Access Card from the computer slot.

The man added, "Credit card and car keys."

She dug out her keys and credit card from her coat pocket. She never bothered with purse or wallet for work because every item on her person was thoroughly searched both coming and going. The company card provided direct access to her per diem account and paid for all her meals, making carrying cash unnecessary. Her personal debit and credit cards were in the townhouse with her passport and other important papers. Because she never needed it on base, she kept her driver's license in the glove box of the company car.

Any phone with a built-in camera was not allowed past security. It was in the phone safe by the security desk, available for use during breaks. She'd be forced to hand that over as they exited the building.

In short, she had no phone, no car, no home, no ID, no credit or debit card, and no cash. Banks were closed today, so she couldn't walk into a branch and withdraw money even if she had ID.

Basically, she was screwed.

Into the phone, she said, "Tim, I don't have any IDs or credit cards or cash. I need to be allowed access to my stuff."

"That's not possible, Leah. Good luck." The line went dead.

"Bastard," she said, barely containing the urge to slam the plastic handset into the cradle. Her hands shook as she grabbed her pathetic few belongings and dumped them in a used FedEx box. The first item to go in was her one framed photo. She stared at her eight-year-old self's gap-toothed grin as she posed with her mother at NASA.

She touched a finger to her mother's forehead. *Sorry I let you down, Mom.*

She turned the photo facedown and tossed a

microwave-safe bowl and a bamboo utensil set she kept in her desk for eating on the fly. Next she grabbed the drawing pad she'd doodled on just minutes ago, then searched the drawers for other personal items. Her favorite ink pen followed the Mt. Vernon ticket into the box. A tube of crimson lipstick rounded out the small pathetic pile, but then, she'd only been here three weeks, and this wasn't the most comfortable of work spaces given the layers of security.

"We need to inspect everything that goes into the box," the male MP said.

She shrugged. "Knock yourself out."

"You can't keep the notebook," the woman said.

"It's just doodles. I draw when I need a brain break."

The woman flipped through the pages. "Looks like a schematic of a computer system to me. You can't take it out of the building."

Leah shrugged, impressed the MP had recognized what it was. It had been worth a try.

The male guard took apart the picture frame and examined every inch of it before dropping the pieces into the box.

"Can I put it back together?"

"No. They'll search it again at the gate."

She sighed.

He lifted the candlelight tour ticket from the box. "We need to copy this."

She nodded. "Go for it. It's invalid after five

forty-five anyway." She glanced at the clock. If she'd left earlier like she wanted to, maybe she would have avoided all this today. It might not be any better tomorrow, but dammit, she'd had plans tonight. And she never had plans.

He copied the ticket while the other MP disassembled the ink pen. The male MP returned and placed the ticket in the box, then he searched her lipstick. In the process, he smashed the waxy compound, making it a misshapen glob. He then scanned her from head to toe. "I'll need to do a pat down."

She raised a brow. "In addition to the scanner at the front of the building?" This office had the same kind of scanners airports had that could identify a hairband left in her pocket.

"Yes. Sorry." His tone said he wasn't, but she'd give him the benefit of the doubt.

She held out her arms, and he performed the pat down. When he was done, he asked if she had any other items for inspection. She handed him her wool coat, and he ran a metal-detecting wand over it, then patted down the liner.

The search was complete just minutes after the two MPs had entered her office. It had happened so quickly, she hadn't quite had time to grasp what this all meant.

She'd just lost…everything. She was being fired from HH after five years. She'd been their star employee, and this assignment had been her crowning achievement. She was no longer working on toys; she was strengthening national security.

But that was all gone now, and her reputation was shot.

There would be no recovering from this, not professionally. And given the classified nature of this work, she wouldn't even be allowed to talk about why she was fired.

The MPs escorted her to the front desk of the building. They retrieved her smartphone from the phone safe and added it to the pile of confiscated items. The door guards repeated the search of her belongings, the pat down, and this time, she got the full-body scan.

Humiliation complete, the MPs escorted her past the front desk—vacant on this December Sunday—and she spotted the landline phone.

She paused. "I need to make a call." Not that she had a clue who she'd call. She had no way to pay for a taxi and didn't have any friends in the area. She'd lived in the DC area for only three weeks and worked alone in what amounted to a cell. Sure, there were supervisors in the outer offices, but she hadn't made friends with any of them.

She'd eaten lunch in the cafeteria several times but hadn't spoken with anyone other than the food service workers.

She considered calling Michelle Hollis, but what could Michelle do? Leah was being fired by the military. Michelle had no say there, and Tim would never get away with confiscating the car and phone if he didn't have Michelle's tacit approval.

"Calls aren't permitted," the male MP said.

A cold calm rage settled in as she left the building and walked toward the base exit, but she held her head high as she crossed through the gate, leaving her life's work and reputation in shambles behind her.

She stood on the sidewalk, next to the wall that defined the naval base. It was a crisp, chill December day. The wind bit into her and whipped at her hair. She didn't have hat, gloves, or scarf because those items were in her company car. She shivered in the wind and wondered what to do next.

She glanced to her right and spotted a beefy SUV parked next to the barricades installed to prevent truck bombs from ramming the base entrance. A man in a dark suit and darker sunglasses leaned casually against the vehicle holding a sign that said simply, "Ellis."

Between the suit and the man's impressive build, he looked more like Secret Service—or maybe mob enforcer—than chauffeur.

She frowned and patted down her pockets for money or phone or credit card she was far too aware weren't there. Assured once again she was shit out of luck, she approached the man with the sign, noting as she did so that with his dark hair, dusky skin, and trim beard, he was attractive.

Her brain screamed this could be some sort of trap, but…did she have any other choice?

He stood with power and authority, his face impassive even though he was surrounded by marines who watched his every move.

That was kinda hot, actually. But then, she'd always had a thing for men who exuded that kind of masculine confidence. It was a shame that in her unfortunate experience, men who exuded alpha pheromones were condescending bastards.

Dex was exhibit A.

But still, this man was nice to look at, and given her day, she could use a little eye candy. If nothing else, it was a pleasant distraction.

"My last name is Ellis. You my ride?" She nodded toward the SUV.

"Depends," the man said, lifting the dark glasses to study her in the cold December sunlight. "Were you just fired?"

She gave him an icy grin. "Lucky me. I was."

He lowered the sunglasses, then folded the handmade sign. "They didn't give me a first name. For what it's worth, I'm sorry. Shitty timing if nothing else."

"Well, this is going to make my New Year's resolutions much easier."

"How so? Going to resolve to get a new job, be a top-notch employee?"

He probably assumed she was guilty of whatever had triggered this abrupt firing. But then, why wouldn't he?

She handed him the FedEx box after plucking her smashed tube of lipstick from inside. "Oh hell no." She applied the bright red color to her lips, then flashed a fast, angry smile. "I was already a top employee. My resolutions will be focused on revenge."

Mr. Hot Driver gave a smile that came and went so fast, she almost thought she'd imagined it, but then he yanked open the rear door of the SUV. "Let's get started, then."

Maybe she did it because she had no choice. Or maybe because she'd been fired without notice on the first night of Hanukkah. Or maybe it was because of that fleeting smile.

She might never fully understand her reason in that moment, but whatever it was, she climbed into the backseat of a car driven by a complete and utter stranger, without knowing his name or who he worked for, knowing full well it could be some sort of trap.

Chapter Two

"Where to?" Nate asked his mysterious passenger with the sexy red lips and cool demeanor.

She wasn't traditionally attractive, her features too asymmetrical, too imperfect with her sharp nose and narrow chin, yet she was…utterly attractive. Stunning even.

She removed her long wool coat before settling into the backseat, and he noted she dressed with a femininity and polish he wouldn't have expected of a military contractor working on the Sunday before Christmas. Pale silk blouse. Blue pencil skirt. Knee-high boots.

Damn. Were knee-high boots ever *not* hot?

She smiled at him in the rearview mirror, unbuttoned the top button of her blouse, and said, "Mt. Vernon."

"What?" He turned in his seat, not wanting to

confine his view to what the rearview allowed. He carefully kept his gaze above her collarbones. He wouldn't take her bait no matter how much cleavage she displayed.

Was it wrong that he was attracted to her on a physical level? After all, the play with the button had been an invitation to notice her, but she could be a traitor to the country he'd served as a Special Forces operator.

"Mt. Vernon. George Washington's plantation. You've heard of it, right?"

"Yes, but—"

"I have a ticket for the holiday candlelight tour. Starts at five forty-five. We'll be early, but maybe I can explore the museum first."

"You want me to take you to Mt. Vernon. After you were fired."

"I bought my ticket weeks ago and have been looking forward to it."

Okay, her cool attitude was kinda hot. And really, if the military suspected her of serious wrongdoing, the MPs wouldn't have stopped at the gate.

"Your choice." He studied the map on the SUV's built-in GPS to refresh his memory, then turned off the screen, put the car in gear, and wove between the bollards to the main road.

He was still learning his way around, but he knew this part of DC. He had a choice between either 395 or 295 to GW Parkway. Habit had him taking the long way, staying on surface streets and conducting a Surveillance Detection Route. Freddy would roll his eyes, wondering why he was making the job take longer than necessary, but he'd have the woman to Mt. Vernon in less than forty-five minutes from the pickup even with the SDR, and it never hurt to practice.

Alaska had been pretty much the worst place to practice this kind of security work. There was only one road into Tamarack, the town closest to the compound, and few roads on the compound itself. In Tamarack, either someone was following you or they already knew where you were going.

If nothing else, the DC area was entertaining, but he was admittedly rusty in this department. There could be a reason other operatives had passed him by in the hierarchy, but he should have been rotated out of Alaska years ago, as he'd repeatedly requested.

He checked the rearview often—no longer focused on his interesting passenger—and noted the vehicles at each intersection. He'd been driving for several minutes when a gray sedan he'd noted twice before appeared a third time. Given his lane changes and turns, that was…odd.

He brushed it off. This was practice, nothing more, but five blocks and two turns later, the car was there again. He tapped his headset to call Josh Warner, an operative who also lived in the Virginia compound. The guy knew about Nate's bonus gig and suggested they both don Raptor headsets in case the contractor turned violent. But really, Nate had figured the former SEAL was bored at the prospect of two weeks off.

"You testing me, man?" He wouldn't put it past Josh to have decided to mess with him. Maybe that was why he'd suggested the headsets to begin with.

"What?"

"Are you on my tail?" Nate asked.

"Hell no. Heading to the gym."

"No tricks? You aren't checking my SDR skills?"

"No way. You suck at SDRs, that's on you. Why? What's going on?"

"Gray sedan has been following me for…two and a half miles. Surface streets, multiple lane changes, and unnecessary turns."

"Not me. Not anyone from Raptor. Sounds like someone is interested in your passenger."

Nate tilted the rearview to center the woman. He didn't even know her first name. She sat forward in her seat, clearly concerned by his conversation. "What's going on?" she asked.

"Thanks, man," he said to Josh and clicked off. To Ellis, he said, "We're being followed."

"By who?" She twisted in her seat to look out the rear window.

"Gray sedan three blocks back. Want me to lose them?"

She turned back to the front. "I have no clue

why anyone would follow us. Hell, I don't even know why I was fired."

He had a hard time believing that, given her cool, controlled demeanor. "So you don't want me to lose them?"

"Not really. I'd like to know who they are. Let them get close."

"I doubt they'd be dumb enough to let you identify them. They're being pretty careful to hang back."

"Well then, lead them to Mt. Vernon. There's only one road in, if I remember correctly. They can't exactly hide."

It wasn't a bad plan, actually. A tourist spot on a Sunday. "You got it. Mind if I bring someone from my team in on this? If they can get behind the gray car, we might get a license plate."

"Your team? I didn't know car services had *teams*."

"I work in private security."

"HH—I presume it was HH and not the government—hired a security guard to drive me around?"

"No, HH hired my brother's car service to take you home. I got roped in to fill in when no one else was available to pick you up today. And sweetheart, I am way more than a security guard."

He caught her smirk in the rearview. "Really? What other services do you provide?" She crossed her legs and leaned back in the seat. "Because I've had to be a good girl since I submitted to the security screen eleven months ago, and about thirty minutes ago, my security clearance stopped mattering. I'm feeling a bit…*reckless*."

Oh hell. This woman was not what he expected. But then, he'd been braced for a weeping victim. "Sadly, I can't help you there. Raptor has a certain professional reputation to uphold."

"You work for *Raptor*?" She said it like an expletive. He really shouldn't find that charming, but given his current frustration, he didn't mind.

"Yep. Going on eight years now. I've been working there since before Senator Ravissant bought the company—back when Robert Beck was CEO." He wasn't entirely sure why he added that, but maybe he was feeling defiant. He was proud of the years he'd given the company. He'd never once done anything to be ashamed of.

"You know the senator?"

"His wife's brother was a close friend." And Vin's death still hurt. He could have done something, if only he'd listened to the soldier. And suddenly, he was reminded he did have something to be ashamed of.

He took another turn, still on the DC side of the Potomac River, going in circles now as the gray car followed them. "Do you want me to bring in another operative or not?"

"Go for it. But you should know, I'm not paying Raptor's fees."

He grinned. "Don't worry, HH is already paying me."

Her eyes flashed with a hint of vicious glee. "By all means, then."

He used his headset to call Josh and invited him out to play. "I'll give you part of my fee," he offered.

"Nah, this is a freebie. Sounds fun. It should take me…twenty minutes to get in place. Head into Alexandria. I'll ping you when it's time to get on GW Parkway."

Nate turned on the GPS screen in anticipation of seeing Josh Warner's vehicle light up on the map. All Raptor vehicles were linked and could track each other, which would allow Josh to find Nate without the need for verbal directions.

Over the headpiece, Josh informed Nate that Chase Johnston had asked to join the game. "Hope you don't mind, Hawk," Chase said, joining the now three-way call. "I'm going to ride shotgun for Josh."

"No problem. The more the merrier."

Once they were in place, Nate took the on-ramp to the parkway and drove direct to George Washington's estate. They reached the parking area and found a spot in the overflow lot, which was only half full. He faced the woman in the backseat. "We can wait here or go inside. Warner and Johnston will get intel on whoever was following you."

She pulled on her coat, then plucked a piece of

paper from the FedEx box on the seat next to her. "I'm early for the candlelight tour, but they'll probably let me explore the museum and grounds." She opened her door and dropped to the pavement.

That was it? They'd been followed and she didn't even give a damn?

Did *he* give a damn?

He could drive off right now and collect an easy grand for his brother. He didn't even need to pass Go.

But something about this didn't sit right with him.

He wrenched open his door and slipped out, catching her before she could walk away. "Wait. You left your box. And I don't even know your name."

She smiled and leaned into him, pressing her hand to his chest where his coat was open. "You work for *Raptor* and haven't tracked down my name yet?"

"Sloppy. I know."

"I'll tell you mine if you tell me yours." Her voice was a husky whisper as she played with a button on his shirt.

He placed a hand over her thick coat, on the small of her back, enjoying this game. She'd gone from attractive and stunning to blazing hot. "Nate. Nate Sifuentes."

"You aren't even going to make me work for it?"

"No. Are you?"

"I think…yes." She rose on her toes and brushed her lips over his. "Thanks for the ride, Nate Sifuentes."

His mind had blanked out at the feel of her in his arms, but the brush of her lips triggered a different reaction.

She slipped from his arms as darkness gathered. The sun was getting ready to set, telling him he'd wasted more time than he'd planned in getting Josh and Chase on board.

"You sure this is where you want to go?" he asked as she walked away. "My brother said you can have me for two hours."

She turned and walked backward. "Two whole hours? We could cover a lot of ground in that time." Her gaze raked him from head to toe. "What's the going rate for two hours with a mercenary?" She glanced at the paper in her hand. "But my ticket is for tonight only. Bummer."

She turned and swayed her hips as she walked into the shadows.

Damn. Well, if nothing else, the job had been interesting. He turned to climb back in the vehicle, when he heard Chase's voice in his headset. "Fifty bucks says she swiped his wallet."

"No way," Josh said. "Nate's a professional. He'd never be taken in by a woman like that."

Nate patted his pocket and felt the blood drain from his face.

Motherfucker.

Chapter Three

*L*eah kept her pace steady as she headed for the visitors' entrance. *Don't look back. Don't act nervous.* She was ninety percent certain he wouldn't cause a scene if she made it inside the building, and with her prepaid ticket, she could cut through the line and disappear onto the plantation grounds. He'd have to buy a ticket—without his wallet.

She was almost home free.

But damn, something about Nate Sifuentes revved her engine.

Now she just had to hope he was the kind of guy who carried cash. Lots of it. Because she needed money to see her through the next few days. She gave thanks for office hijinks at tech companies that taught her the skill of lifting wallets. It had been two decades since she'd tried it, but apparently, it was like riding a bicycle—when you were desperate enough.

She followed the path that cut through the trees and reached the brick sidewalk that fronted the restaurant. Escape was in sight.

The roar of an engine made her stop in her tracks. She turned toward the sound, and headlights flared, blinding her.

Before she could blink, a body slammed into her, pushing her away from the road, toward the trees. She hit the ground, landing on bricks with a heavy body on top of her. With her peripheral vision, she saw a blur of a car jump the curb and race along the brick walkway where she'd just been standing. Tires screeched as the car lurched back to the road, disappearing as it sped into the darkness.

She turned her face back to the bricks, her cheek pressed against the cold hard clay, a man's body pressed to hers in the gathering darkness as other pedestrians shouted and screamed.

Her heart raced as she breathed in the scent of dirt and mortar and brick and burnt rubber.

What the hell had just happened?

From the shouts, she gathered that no one else had been in the path of the vehicle. She'd been alone on that stretch of sidewalk and had been saved by the shove that pushed her to the tree line.

She nudged the man who protected her body with his own. The man who'd just saved her life. His weight shifted, and she turned to face him, panting, her heart racing, even though she'd exerted nothing.

She met Nate Sifuentes's gaze. Her heart squeezed at the look in his beautiful brown eyes. "Thank you."

"You going to tell me your name now?"

"Leah. Leah Ellis."

"Maybe—and I'm just spitballing here—you'd have been better off if you worried more about the guy tailing us instead of stealing my wallet."

Her mind was a jumble of adrenaline and fear. He was right, of course, but who was to say Nate wasn't working with the guy who'd tried to run her down? All she could do was nod.

"You two okay?" a man asked from several feet away.

She pushed at Nate's chest.

He shifted his weight and stood, then offered her a hand. She took it, and he pulled her to her feet.

To the Good Samaritan, she said, "I think so. Just rattled." She glanced around the sidewalk. The car was long gone. "What happened?"

"It looked like some idiot ran the stop sign, then swerved to avoid an oncoming car," the man said.

An accident? Nothing but freakish timing? Did she really believe that?

"Did you get the license plate?" Nate asked.

"It all happened too fast," the man said. He turned back to the restaurant. "Glad you're okay.

You should check with security. Maybe they have a camera and got the plate."

"Will do," Nate said. "Thanks."

Alone again on the sidewalk, Nate turned to her. "We'll report this, but first I want some answers. What are you involved in? Why were we followed?"

"I don't know." She gazed at the road where the car had disappeared. She realized she still clutched her candlelight tour ticket in her hand and shoved it into the inside pocket of her coat, next to Nate's wallet. The extra QR code printed on the ticket could be more valuable than she realized.

"Why did you rob me, Leah?"

She decided to give him the truth. "Because I'm scared. And I didn't know if I could trust you."

His mouth flattened, but he didn't argue her point. "Why?" he asked.

She glanced down, unwilling to look at his face, not wanting to be swayed by his handsome features. Just because he was hot didn't mean he was trustworthy. Instead, she inspected her skirt, noting a small split at the side seam. That was the problem with pencil skirts. No room to run.

She'd have worn jeans today if she'd known it was firing day. Instead, she'd dressed for the candlelight tour in an outfit that made her feel pretty and feminine and maybe a bit sexy. Because she never had plans. Never did anything for herself, and on this, the first night of Hanukkah, she wanted to feel like she was part of the world. To be a tourist, then go home and light the menorah and think about her mom and miraculous light that vanquished the darkness.

Ten days from her New Year's resolution to work less and enjoy life more and dammit, her life had imploded.

"Why, Leah?" Nate repeated, his voice soft. Concerned. Forcing her to face the nightmare instead of focusing on the rip in her skirt.

She met his gaze. "Why? You're working for HH. I don't know you. You're a mercenary. And by your own admission, you proudly worked for a traitor."

He cocked his head at her and raised a brow. "What?"

"Your boss is a bad, bad man."

"For the record, I work for Raptor, not HH. And Keith Hatcher might play favorites, but he's a good man."

"I'm talking about Robert Beck. You said you worked for him."

"Years ago."

"Yeah. But still. You specifically mentioned him."

His eyes flattened. "He signed my paycheck. That's all."

"Fine. But I still don't know you." She again looked toward where the car had sped away. "And I'm scared."

An SUV stopped in the roadway in front of them. "Sifuentes," a man shouted, "Need a ride to your car?"

Nate met her gaze. "That's Josh. He's on my team. Will you get in the car with us so we can figure out what's going on?"

She held his gaze. She had nowhere else to turn. She gave him a sharp nod. "But I keep your wallet. Until I feel safe."

The woman had ovaries, he'd give her that. He had the upper hand, but she was cutting deals. He figured he could handle losing forty bucks cash, and there was no avoiding Josh and Chase sharing the tale of how he'd let a woman pick his pocket using the oldest trick in the book.

He wanted answers, so he agreed to her terms.

They climbed into the back of the SUV. "Did you get the license plate?" he asked as they pulled away from the curb.

"No. Too many cars between us, and the glimpses we got showed it was mud splattered. If you'd stayed in the overflow lot instead of walking out to the road, we might have been able to move closer."

Leah leaned back in the seat and glared at Josh's back. She didn't like his mild reprimand.

"Why'd you bolt?" Chase asked her.

She met Chase's gaze, and her face softened. He had that effect on women. It was like they could sense how he'd suffered, and given his boyish face, they wanted to protect him.

She dropped her gaze to her hands, which were on her lap, fingers intertwined. Knuckles white. "I was in a car with a complete stranger. I didn't know if he was bullshitting about someone following us. For all I know, he made it up so he could bring you guys in and I'd blindly play along."

"Why would he do that?" Chase asked, a genuine question in his tone.

She cocked her head. "Do you guys know what I do for a living?"

"Up until an hour or so ago, you were a contractor at the Navy Yard," Josh said as the SUV parked next to Nate's vehicle. "Your official employer is HH, the toy drone company."

"I was writing code for military drones at the Navy Yard. That's all I'm allowed to say—the contract is public knowledge—and with that information alone, there are reasons people might think it beneficial to kidnap me."

She met Chase's gaze again. "The MPs confiscated my company phone, my company car, and the NSA is locking down my company-provided home. I have no money. No ID. No place to sleep, and no one to call in the DC area. I'm utterly vulnerable and shouldn't even be telling you guys this because you could be kidnapping me right now."

"Holy shit," Nate muttered. He'd had no idea. He forgave her for stealing his wallet.

"You think that's why you were given the boot?" Chase asked. "So someone could grab you when you're vulnerable like this?"

"The car that nearly ran her down wasn't trying to abduct her," Nate said. "It was trying to kill her."

"Or maybe just scare me." She sucked in a sharp breath. "So I'd get in the car with you." Her voice held alarm. In a flash, she yanked on the door handle and tumbled out of the SUV. She hit the ground running, heading toward the lights and people in the main lot.

Nate scrambled across the seat and followed through the open door. He couldn't let her take off like this, and not because she had his wallet. She needed help.

She couldn't run in the pencil skirt, and he caught her easily. She fought him, shoving at his arms and trying to scratch him. He trapped her by wrapping his arms around her, imprisoning her in an embrace that wouldn't hurt her or allow her to hurt him. But he felt like an ass for doing it when she was so clearly panicked.

"Shhhh," he whispered, as if he were calming a feral cat. Not that any feral cat was ever calmed by being shushed. But he didn't know what else to do. To say.

Josh and Chase had wisely stayed in the car. Thank God. If all three of them had come after her, he had no doubt she'd be even more terrified.

"I won't hurt you, Leah," he whispered. "I'm not after you. I have no loyalty to HH. I am, however, loyal to my country—I served for twelve years in the Army and was a Green Beret—but I know that if the US military thought you were stealing secrets, you'd be in a cell right now, not at Mt. Vernon. So I'm going to trust you and want to help you. Can you trust me?"

She stopped struggling and met his gaze. Her eyes still held a hint of a feral gleam, but she was calmer. "I don't know."

"What if I let you drive the SUV? Would you feel better then?" Jesus, he could get fired for letting her drive the company car, but right now, he didn't care.

"Where would we go?" she asked.

"That's up to you."

"I…have money. In the bank, I mean. Lots of it. I just can't access my money until my bank opens tomorrow. And even then, I might not be able to make a withdrawal without ID, but I could transfer money to you online if you let me use your phone. I'll pay you double your expenses." She tucked her head against his chest. "This sounds like a con—but it's not."

"I know. And you don't need to pay me to help you. I'm not doing this for the money."

She pushed at his chest. "If not for the money, why did you pick me up? Does Raptor want me for something? I'm not a hacker—white hat or otherwise. I won't be anyone's pawn."

"No! I didn't mean it that way. Initially, yeah, picking you up was for the money. My brother is getting a cool grand for what's supposed to be an hour or two of work. But this, now, helping you—I don't care about money."

"Then why are you doing it?"

"Because I see a scared woman in a desperate situation. No phone, no money, no home, no car? What kind of asshole does that? And to do it when the weather is freezing, on a Sunday, right before the holidays. It's just wrong." He loosened his hold, resisting the urge to cup her cheek, because she'd probably take it the wrong way given his next words. "Where did you plan to sleep tonight?"

She shrugged. "No clue."

"I can't take you home with me. I live in the Raptor compound, and while they're lenient on a lot of things, bringing a person with your kind of computer skills—after you've been fired by the DoD —into the compound would be seen as a huge security risk. I'm already not employee of the month, so I'd be fired in a heartbeat. But I can get you a hotel room for the night."

"Thank you. I'll pay you back." Her features were visible in the glow of the streetlamp. The hard edges remained and he could still feel the tension in her body as he held her, but the slightly haunted look had disappeared.

She smiled. It wasn't a particularly warm or friendly smile, but it was her smile, the one she'd given him before vowing revenge and climbing into his SUV. She was in control again, and as before, something stirred in his chest. He nodded toward his SUV. "Let's go."

"You'll let me drive?" she asked as she approached the driver's side.

"As long as you tell me where we're going."

She climbed in. He circled to the passenger seat and tapped his headphone and told Josh and Chase the plan. "Follow, but hang back, watch our six."

"You got it. Where we headed?"

He looked at Leah. "Where are we going?"

"I want to drive by the townhouse. See if the NSA is there. Maybe someone will give me my wallet."

"That could mean picking up a tail again. The last one tried to run you down."

"Then we won't drive directly to the townhouse. There's a playground a few blocks away. I'll park there." She hit the power button on the dash and the engine came on. "Should I drive straight to the playground?"

"Might as well. No point in wasting time. Where is the townhouse?"

"In Arlington."

Nate relayed the address she provided to Josh

and they set out. The drive would take at least twenty-five minutes. He used the time to study Leah, while also keeping an eye out for a tail.

"You're staring at me," she said.

"You're nice to look at."

She rolled her eyes even as she smiled and kept her gaze on the road ahead. "I don't for a second believe that's why you're watching me."

"Sweetheart, you stole my wallet with the faintest of kisses. I think you know your appeal."

"That was kind of fun."

He laughed. "Only kind of?"

She grinned. "Fine. My heart was beating so fast, it was a wild rush."

"That's more like it. You know what else is a wild rush?"

She snorted, and he let out a sharp laugh. She was relaxing, and that was his goal. He wasn't fishing for compliments.

Not really.

But damn, he had a thing for supergenius computer programmers with badass boots and a matching demeanor.

His cell phone rang. He checked caller ID and saw it was his brother. He debated for a moment, then hit the button to send the call to voicemail. He was going off book on a job with one of Freddy's better clients. Best not to talk to him while Leah was driving his car.

"So…you said earlier you've had to be a good girl for the last eleven months?"

"I was trying to be provocative."

"It worked. Is it true?"

She gave a little noncommittal shrug and said, "Yes."

"Bummer."

"I survived." Then she added in a whisper, "Barely."

"I lived in a remote area in Alaska for six years. Pretty much the only available woman in town was in love with my boss, the compound director." He smiled thinking about Jenna and Brad, who'd gotten married two years ago. Tamarack had treated it like a royal event and celebrated for three days. "You think eleven months is bad. Try living in Alaska."

"Oh my." She kept her gaze on the road, but he saw the side-eye. "You're being awfully frank."

"I want you to trust me."

"I appreciate that." He caught her faint smile. "How long have you been in the DC area?"

"Six months. You?"

"Three weeks. I moved here for the contract, which was supposed to last six months, with possible extensions."

"Where are you from?"

"For the last five years, Philadelphia. I grew up in Illinois, worked in tech on the West Coast, then got the job with HH and moved east."

"Where'd you go to school?"

"Did a one-year technical college right after high school. No fancy degree for me. You were in the Army?"

"Yes. I did community college for a year after high school, then joined the Army. Left when Robert Beck offered me a job. I worked on the Hawaii compound for two years before being sent to Alaska to molder."

"Was Alaska that bad?"

"Yes and no. There's a lot I love about the place. Heck, I'd live there again. There's nothing like the aurora borealis in February. The mountains and forests. But...I was alone. Within the first year, I dated pretty much all the single women within a fifty-mile radius, and no relationship clicked. At first, the lack of options didn't matter to me—I didn't think I wanted to get married, have kids. But the longer I was there, the more I felt like life was passing me by—like how would I know what I want without the opportunity to meet people? I started asking to transfer to DC so I could be near my brother and his family, but the Alaska compound was in turmoil around the time Rav was elected to the Senate, so they kept me there. Finally made parole six months ago."

"You like it here?"

"I like the area, yes. Not feeling great about my job with Raptor these days, to be honest. The only position they'd give me here was a live-in job on the compound, but I'm done with compound life. Cameras everywhere. Intense security. Been there, done that."

"Sounds like my work. I was searched coming and going, every day. Fishbowl office. Wasn't allowed a cell phone past security. It was such a pain to leave the building to have lunch in the cafeteria, I ate at my desk more often than not. Three weeks in DC and you're the first person besides my supervisor I've actually had a conversation with."

"Damn."

She made a face. "I was so looking forward to the candlelight tour. I mean, it's silly because I was going by myself. But at least I'd be around people. Living."

"I'm sorry you missed it."

"But look at me, having a conversation with another person, like a real human. I mean, forget the fact you might've abducted me and I just haven't realized it yet."

"I haven't abducted you. I promise. I've almost never abducted anyone in my whole life."

"Almost never doesn't sound as promising as you think."

"It was a mission. Classified, but I'll say we found a woman hemorrhaging after childbirth when we were sent in to rescue American soldiers. She would have died if we didn't take her too."

"Okay, that sounds fair."

She exited the highway a mile from the address

she'd given him. "So what's the plan here, Nate? This is your specialty, not mine. Drive straight to the park or take a twisted route?"

"Go straight there. No one except Josh is following us."

She pulled into the parking lot of the playground and put the SUV in Park. She kept her hands on the steering wheel, gripping it like it was a lifeline. "Can I get in trouble for just being here when the NSA has seized the place?"

"I don't know, but as long as you don't try to enter, I don't see a problem. Let's scout it out, then decide what to do."

"People don't really walk in this neighborhood at night. Not unless they have a dog."

"No time to adopt a puppy. We'll just have to hold hands. A couple out looking for Christmas lights. Sound good?"

"Fine."

He radioed Josh and Chase and told them the plan. They parked a few blocks on the other side of the townhouse, at a strip mall. Nate then pulled the headset down and slipped it under his collar. The microphone could still pick up his words but remained out of sight. For now, he turned off the mic.

The headset operated with both radio and cell when they needed to cover greater distance. It had a broadcast cell feature, which meant every operative all over the world could listen in if their headset was on, but tonight he'd been using it as a simple cell with three-way calling to communicate with Josh and Chase.

Nate circled the vehicle and took Leah's hand. Her grip was firm, a sign of just how worried she was knowing she still believed he might be a threat. Or maybe their conversation during the drive had managed to ease her fears.

Her boots made a solid tapping sound on the cold pavement as their breath billowed out in white puffs. The temperature had taken a nosedive now that the sun was down. She shivered—and he was pretty sure it was with cold, not fear—and leaned into him, drawn by his body heat. "Damn. I wish I had my hat, scarf, and gloves."

"Our next stop will be a store." If he'd been thinking, they'd have gone to the store first.

"Thank you."

They reached the main driveway that fronted the townhouse complex. "The HH townhouse is on the last street in the back of the neighborhood."

The roads twisted and turned, wrapping around with multiple four-house rows facing each other. With the curves of the streets, they wouldn't see her unit until they were almost upon it. Not ideal for a casual walk, but really, they weren't doing anything *wrong*. Just checking out her home.

A sidewalk paralleled the roadway and veered into trees planted to look as if the complex had trails, but there was far more pavement than trees, and it wasn't the sort of place where people indulged in casual strolls. So very different from Alaska.

They finally neared her unit, and he led her into the shadows where the sidewalk crisscrossed beneath the trees. He leaned back against a trunk, pulling her into his arms.

"What are you doing?" she asked.

"Casing your townhouse." He unbuttoned his coat and pressed her to his chest, wrapping her in his warmth. His lips found her neck, and he whispered in her ear, "If anyone spots us, I'm taking advantage of the darkness to make out with a beautiful woman."

She melted into him, playing along, but he guessed she also appreciated the shared body heat. "What do you see?"

His mouth moved along her neck as his gaze swept the row of houses. "No car in your driveway. No one sitting in any parked cars on the street." There were four three-story townhomes on each block. "Lower floor is garage and utilities?"

"Yes. Middle is living, kitchen, office, and half bath. Top is two bedrooms, two bath."

"Sounds nice. Let me tell you about my dorm room sometime."

She let out a small huff of a laugh. She felt a little too good in his arms like this.

He focused on the job. The unit on the end was dark, but the other three were lit on their middle and top floors. One unit had a menorah in the window, with two candles lit. He glanced at Leah's unit again and realized the dark shape in the living room window was a menorah. "I thought Hanukkah didn't start until tomorrow?"

"Most calendars mark the first full day of Hanukkah, but it really starts at sunset the night before." She twisted to be able to see the row of houses. "I'd better get my menorah back. It was my mother's."

He pulled her tighter against him. "I'll do what I can to help you get it back." He meant it. This wasn't a job anymore. He wanted to help this woman. And not just because she turned him on.

She turned back and cupped his face, her fingers caressing his beard. "I appreciate your help. Especially after I stole your wallet."

He patted his inside breast pocket—he'd gotten it back when she first took over driving—and made a show of being relieved to find it there even with her wrapped in his coat.

Headlights flashed the trees, then turned down the drive. He placed a hand behind her head and pulled her close, kissing her to conceal both their faces as the lights washed over them.

She opened her mouth, taking the kiss deeper than necessary, but maybe she didn't know the rules of stage kissing for cover. He couldn't really find it in him to complain about her technique as her tongue slipped inside his mouth and stroked his in a kiss that sent heat billowing through his body.

The night was no longer cold and dark. It was ablaze with bright flames that threatened to consume him. The car passed them by, but the kiss continued. He nibbled her lips, traced her mouth with his tongue. Tasted. Teased. And basically forgot everything except her mouth. Her body hot against his. The soft sounds of pleasure she made. With his back to the tree, he widened his stance, and she settled between his legs, pressing into his erection. Making it clear this kiss wasn't an act.

She pulled away, sucked in a deep breath, and muttered, "Damn." Then she met his gaze. "I mentioned it's been over eleven months, right?"

He tucked her hair behind an ear. "You did. It's been nearly two years for me."

"No way! I thought, now that you aren't in Alaska…"

He shrugged. "I've gone on a few dates, but none that made me want to get physical. After making a habit of one-night stands whenever I traveled, seeking sex for sex's sake lost its appeal. If I'm going to be inside someone, I want spark."

"And was that spark?" she asked, her eyes bright with mischief.

"Oh honey, that was a damn inferno." He leaned down and kissed her again, thankful this wasn't a Raptor job. With Raptor, there were rules against this kind of thing. But his brother had never said anything about not getting it on with the clients. Not that he'd care if Freddy had.

She opened her mouth and let him inside, making a small purring sound as he explored her hot, delicious depths.

And to think he'd wanted to shoot Freddy with paintballs when he'd woken him this morning.

A scent caught his nose, and he kept kissing her, savoring her taste, before it finally registered. He raised his head. "Is that smoke?"

She stiffened and twisted in his arms, turning toward her townhouse. There was a definite glow behind the living room window.

"*No,*" she whispered.

He cursed, pulled out his cell phone, and dialed 911. "Why isn't an alarm going off?" he asked as he waited for the call to connect.

"I don't know. It has a top-of-the-line system."

The operator picked up, and he reported the fire. As he watched, the glow flashed, illuminating the dark menorah in bright orange light.

"We need to warn the neighbors!" She bolted from their spot in the trees and ran as fast as her skirt would allow, shouting, "Fire!" as she ran.

He darted past her, heading for the unit next to hers. "Fire!" He pounded on the door. "Fire!" He ran to the next unit as she caught up with him and took over pounding on the first door.

He was at the door of the third occupied house when people began pouring from the units. Sirens sounded in the distance. The family in the unit closest to hers gathered on the street clutching a few random items—a computer, a photo album, and a stuffed animal were in the teenager's hands. His younger sister held a bird cage and the family dog's leash. The bird flapped against the bars as the dog barked. Both mothers had purses slung over their shoulders as they held their children and stared at the glow of flames and smoke that threatened their home.

"We should pull the car out of the garage," the teenager said.

"Too much risk. The gas furnace could blow," one of the moms said.

After giving Josh and Chase an update, Nate turned to see Leah staring at the burning townhouse. He draped an arm around her. "Do you have a lot of personal items inside?" Given that it was just a temporary home, he could hope.

She leaned into him. "The furniture all belongs to HH. The only items I brought with me are the personal items I can't live without."

Only the items that were most important to her, like her mother's menorah.

He tightened his grip on her as his heart splintered. "I'm so sorry, sweetheart."

"Excuse me?" one of the neighbors asked. "Are you the woman who lived there?"

"Yes."

"How did the fire start?"

"I don't know. We weren't inside. We were over there"—she pointed to the trees where they'd kissed—"when we saw the flames."

The fire engines arrived with blaring sirens, preventing all further conversation. The crowd was pushed to the far end of the row of houses, away from the blazing unit. In the dark shadows at the very end, Nate pulled her aside and whispered in her ear, "We need to get you out of here, now."

"But won't that look suspicious?"

"You're already going to be the prime suspect. NSA is supposed to search the place, and now it's burning. They're going to think you set the fire to destroy evidence. And if you're taken into custody, it's going to be that much harder to figure out what's going on."

He took her hand, pulled her onto a path that ran beside the far end of the rows of homes, and tapped his mic. "Get in position on the main road. We're going to cut through the woods."

"On our way."

He then bent down, pulled open her jacket, and ripped the seam of her skirt open to the upper thigh. "We're going to run along the far side of the development, away from the driveway and path, and meet up with Josh down the road."

She nodded and took off, running across the grass that flanked the development. He ran behind her. They'd just reached a thin band of woods that separated the development from the main road when the police arrived. Thank goodness for her dark coat, boots, and hair.

He spotted Josh's SUV through the trees and directed her to stay in the woods until they were on top of it. "Open the door," he said into the headset, and the moment they left the woods, it popped open. Nate dove in first, then turned and grabbed Leah, pulling her inside as Josh gunned the engine and they leapt from the curb.

Chapter Four

*L*eah's heart beat like a death metal tune. She leaned against Nate in the backseat, his arms still around her, her jacket open and skirt split to her upper thigh. She tried not to think about her belongings going up in flames. Maybe the firefighters would put it out before everything was lost.

Nate's arms tightened, and she wanted to sink into his warmth and forget she'd just run from a burning townhouse that held her most precious mementos and she'd likely face arson charges.

"I didn't do it," she muttered.

"You've got an alibi. Me. And Chase and Josh."

"But what if they say you're in on it with me? Or I managed to set it up to burn before I left the house this morning?"

"Because you knew you were going to be fired? And I'd never seen you before in my life until you walked through the gate at the Navy Yard. We've had no contact. There is no way I can be implicated in this."

"You just helped me escape when my home was burning."

"Because I have grounds to believe you're in danger and I work in security—this is exactly my field. Don't forget, someone tried to run you down at Mt. Vernon before we found the townhouse on fire."

"But we didn't report what happened at Mt. Vernon to the police."

"Wrong," Josh said from the front seat. "I called it in while you were talking in the parking lot. I said you were too rattled to make a statement but that you were okay. They've got cameras by the visitor center. They'll have enough information for a report."

She pulled away from Nate's arms and tugged at her skirt, trying to recover a bit of dignity as she was reminded of the two other men in the car. "Thank you. I should have thought of calling the police."

"You had other fears front and center." To Josh, Nate said, "Take us to my SUV—but drive by first. Make sure it's clear."

They circled the park. "Where will you go?" Josh asked.

"Don't know," Nate said. "Somewhere underground."

"Raptor's got the safe house in Annandale," Josh suggested.

"Can't get Raptor involved in that way. I can jeopardize my security clearance, but not the company's. Keith would have my ass."

"Keith wouldn't—" Josh said.

Chase interrupted. "Gotcha covered, Hawk. I rented a cabin near Shenandoah for the holidays. It's been mine since yesterday, but with the party and all, I'd decided not to head out until Christmas Eve." He held up his phone. "I just texted you the directions and the code for the key box. It's about two hours from here. You'll need to pick up groceries and stuff. There's a kitchen with the basics, but no food."

She looked to Nate to see what he'd say, and relief fluttered through her as he reached between the seats to shake Chase's hand. "Thanks, man. I owe you."

She leaned between the seats and kissed his cheek. "I don't even know you. I hardly know what to say."

"You're going to be stuck with Negative Nate in a remote cabin. Try not to kill him. Or if you do, don't stain the carpet. It's a hefty deposit."

She laughed.

Chase glanced at her ripped skirt. "You'll need clothes too. There's snow on the ground at the cabin."

Josh drove them back to the park, and they

jumped from the SUV without lingering. In moments, they were back on the road with Nate at the wheel and Josh following several blocks behind as they wound through surface streets before getting on the highway and heading southwest.

"Josh is watching pinch points to see if we're being tailed. We can't go shopping until we're certain we're clear. We'll find a Target or something on the way, so we can get clothes and food."

They spent twenty minutes driving in circles, then were cut free by Josh. No tail. She settled back in the seat as they took the on-ramp for 66. "That was really kind of Chase," she said.

"Extremely generous considering he rented this place because his cabin burned down in October."

"That's awful!" And then she remembered all her belongings were probably ash and cinders, and she could guess why Chase hadn't hesitated. "What happened?"

"It's a long, ugly story and not mine to share beyond saying it was arson and no one was hurt. But someday maybe Chase will tell you."

"You say that like you think we're going to be friends after this."

He gave her a sideways glance. She could just make out his soft expression in the glow of the dashboard lights. "I think that's inevitable."

Suddenly, she remembered their kiss. The very real kiss that had her wanting to drop her panties in the trees next to the townhouse.

She had plenty of sexual experience and couldn't think of a single kiss that had affected her like that before. As Nate said, it had been inferno hot.

She wasn't sure if "friends" was the right word to describe what they'd be when all this was over, but she hoped that was at least part of it.

Thirty miles from Arlington, they found a Target. It was nine p.m., one hour before closing. Her belly rumbled as they entered the grocery section of the store, and she realized she hadn't eaten anything since the protein bar she'd had for lunch.

Tonight, she'd planned to have brisket and latkes. Knowing she wouldn't be home until after the candlelight tour, she'd cooked the brisket last night while she worked on Peacemaker for HH. She immediately began gathering ingredients to make latkes and found a premade brisket. It would have to do.

Nate didn't say anything as she added items to the cart, he just added his own selections—bread, milk, eggs, cheese, apples. She grabbed a premade chicken sandwich from the deli—a snack to tide them over on the drive—then, after grabbing toothbrushes, toothpaste, and other toiletries, they moved on to the clothing section, where she selected yoga pants and jeans and a few tops along with socks, underwear, and tennis shoes.

The only item she bothered to try on were the

shoes, being careful to remove the boots without opening her coat and showing off the slit in the skirt. Nate grabbed a few items of clothing too, then they moved on to find hats and gloves for both of them. They were heading toward checkout when they passed the holiday section, and she stopped in her tracks.

As to be expected on the first night of Hanukkah, the shelf with menorahs and candles had been thoroughly picked over. The menorahs that remained were substandard. The shamash was the same height as the other eight holders. And the boxes of thirty-minute candles were down to the dregs. Through the plastic window, she could see broken candle after broken candle.

By the time they got to the cabin and she could light the menorah, it would be around eleven. So very late. But better late than never.

She grabbed a substandard menorah with the wrong shamash and put it in the cart along with three boxes of candles. Surely there'd be some whole ones in there. She looked up and met Nate's gaze, remembering that he was paying for all this. "Do you mind?"

"Of course not." He put another box of candles in the cart. "Do you need anything else?"

She looked at the bucket full of dreidels and the bags of chocolate gelt. She started to shake her head, but he smiled and put one of each in the cart.

They moved on, passing one of the many

Christmas aisles, and it was his turn to pause. "We'll probably be there for a few days." He grabbed a knit red, white, and green stocking from a hook and put it in the cart.

"You should get one for Chase too. He said he's coming Christmas Eve."

"Good idea." He grabbed a few bags of candy. "Gotta have something to put in them." He then topped off the pile with a string of colored lights.

By the time they reached the cashier, the cart was quite full, but for someone who had lost everything in a matter of hours, she felt surprisingly light.

She'd seen her mother's menorah in a house being consumed by fire. In an instant, she'd felt cut off from the past, cut off from her mother, as if her death happened yesterday and not a year ago, but with the simple act of purchasing a new menorah, she was reminded that as long as she carried on the traditions, she would always have a connection to the past, both to her mother and the ancestors who came before.

No one could take that from her.

They quickly loaded their purchases in the rear compartment of the SUV and were back on the road. They split the sandwich as Nate drove. When they were done eating, he asked her about possible reasons she'd been fired.

"I missed a deadline on Friday, but the captain overseeing my project told me it wasn't a problem. He's out until after Christmas anyway. And even if

it were an issue, firing me is extreme. I'm baffled."
And then there had been the car that tried to run
her down, and the burning townhouse.

None of it made sense.

She closed her eyes. She'd been feeling good
after their retail therapy and wanted to forget, even
if just for a few hours. "Tell me about Alaska. I've
always wanted to visit."

He launched into stories about forty-degrees-
below cold, and her heart surged with affection for
this stranger who understood her need to escape
without her having to explain.

It felt like almost no time had passed by the time
they navigated the twisty mountain road to the
resort that rented out at least a dozen cabins. Each
one was tucked in the woods and appeared
secluded. Utterly private. Chase had called ahead to
let the owners know of their late arrival, and they'd
sent someone over to build a fire so the cabin
wouldn't be cold.

She felt a rush of bubbly heat as the headlights
washed over the one-bedroom cabin she would
share with the mysterious stranger who'd rescued
her today. It was cozy. Picturesque. And with snow
on the ground and smoke billowing from the chim-
ney, utterly romantic.

They unloaded their purchases along with her
FedEx box. Clothing and toiletries were unceremo-
niously dumped in the bedroom and groceries piled
on the kitchen island.

Done with the repeat trips to the car, she peeled off her coat and hung it on the hook by the door. She still wore the ripped skirt and, when she caught the heat in Nate's eyes as his gaze traveled up her boot to her bare thigh, she decided to keep it on while she made the latkes and heated up the brisket.

But before she could cook, she needed to light the menorah. She reassembled the picture frame from the FedEx box and put it next to the menorah on the table, glad to have a photo of her mother with her. After turning off the side-table lamps that flanked the living room window, she opened a box of candles and found two whole ones, then glanced over her shoulder to where Nate was adding a log to the fire. "Join me?" she asked.

He smiled. "I'd be honored." He closed the grate and crossed to stand beside her. "I've never done this before."

"You know the story, right? How the oil lasted for eight days?"

"The basics, yes."

"Tomorrow night, when we do this right—thirty minutes after sunset—I can tell you the whole thing. We'll keep it simple tonight."

She placed the first candle in the holder on the right end and the shamash in the center, then said the Hanukkah blessing. "*Baruch atah, Adonai Eloheinu, Melech haolam, asher kid'shanu b'mitzvotav v'tsivanu l'hadlik ner shel Hanukkah.*" She translated for Nate. "Blessed are You, Adonai our God, Sovereign of all, who hallows us with mitzvot, commanding us to kindle the Hanukkah lights." Then she said the first night blessing and translated it as well, adding, "We only say that one on the first night of Hanukkah."

She struck a match on the side of the box and caught the whiff of sulfur as the flame flared. She held the match to the shamash, then shook out the match and set it aside. She lifted the shamash from its holder and used it to light the first candle, replacing it in the center when done. She stepped back and looked at the teardrop flames and said, "Let's put it in the window."

She lifted the menorah by its heavy base and decided it wasn't such a bad little menorah after all. The smell of melting wax, the flicker of flame, the spoken blessings that invoked the past—it was all that was needed to make any menorah special.

She set it in the front window and stepped back. Nate turned out the overhead lights in the adjacent kitchen, making the glow of the fire and the two small candles the only light in the connected rooms. He stood behind her, looking over her shoulder toward the candles in the window.

"My dad left when I was about five," she said. "I was an only child, so it was just my mom and me growing up. She was pretty secular when it came to Judaism, but she always said the traditions are important. They connect us to our history. This is the first Hanukkah since Mom died last December."

His arms surrounded her as he pulled her back to his chest, his muscled forearms crossed over her breastbone as he wrapped her in his warmth. "I'm sorry for your loss."

"Thank you." She reached up and hooked her hands over his crossed arms, holding him in place, thankful for his encompassing embrace. "And thank you for being with me right now. I was dreading being alone when I lit the candles."

His lips brushed her temple. "You can have me all eight nights."

"You're a good man, Negative Nate."

He laughed. "I was wondering how long it would be before you brought that up."

She wanted to stand like this forever, but she had latkes to make, so she pulled away, giving up his heat in exchange for getting to look at his face, which was, she confirmed, still incredibly handsome. She brushed her lips over his. "I'm going to demand the whole story over dinner."

"It's nothing." He stroked her cheek, tucking her hair behind an ear. "I'm not feeling all that negative right now."

"Well, that's because I make the best latkes in the world."

"Yeah. That's the reason."

She pulled away—reluctantly—and crossed to the small kitchen.

"How long do we leave the candles burning?"

"We can't blow them out. They have to burn

down. The candles are supposed to last thirty minutes. Bigger—longer-lasting—candles are only used on the last night."

She set to work in the kitchen as Nate called Josh and Chase to give them an update. "Thank Chase profusely for me," she said as she shredded the potatoes.

Nate explored the small cabin as he talked, disappearing into the bedroom, then she heard the sliding glass door open. He must be checking out the back deck.

He returned to the kitchen a few minutes later, phone tucked away. "Did you know this place has a hot tub?"

"Really?"

"After dinner, want to sit outside in the tub and look for shooting stars?"

She cocked her head. "I didn't buy a suit."

"Neither did I." He grinned. "I'll close my eyes coming and going."

"Do I have to close my eyes too?"

He flexed his arms, showing off his impressive muscles. "Not if you don't want to."

She had no doubt that if she got into the tub with him, they'd have sex. Maybe not tonight—after all, she was exhausted and imagined he was too—but naked-hot-tub time was definitely foreplay.

She reminded herself that she'd been a good girl for the last year because she'd needed to pass—

and maintain—the highest level of security clearance. She'd been prepared to behave for the full six months she'd expected to be working at the Navy Yard.

Now it was moot. There was no reason not to indulge.

Her earlier fears—that he was part of whatever was going on—had evaporated. Maybe that made her a fool, but it wasn't like she had anyone else she could turn to.

"Can I help?" he asked, nodding toward the ingredients spread across the counter.

"Nah. This is a one-butt kitchen. But you can pour the wine."

He poured them each a glass, and she sipped as she worked, enjoying this far more than seemed reasonable, considering he was a stranger and the day she'd had. But she was going to stop questioning it.

"Why don't you hang the stockings by the fireplace?" she asked.

"In my family, we don't hang stockings until Christmas Eve. Then it's time to read 'A Visit from St. Nicholas,' set out cookies for Santa, and off to bed. My family is more Santa-focused than religious. Christmas is about the lights and the tree and food and family."

She could relate to that. "What were—are—your plans this year?" She shouldn't assume he'd changed his plans in the few hours of their acquaintance, even if he'd offered to be by her side for all eight nights of Hanukkah.

"I was going to spend Christmas Eve and Day at my brother's house. He's got six-year-old twins— a boy and a girl. I was looking forward to watching them get caught up in the excitement."

Much as she didn't want to be alone in the coming days, she couldn't be selfish. "You can still join them."

He smiled and crossed the room, then set his wineglass on the kitchen island and pulled her against him. With one hand, he lifted her chin and pressed a kiss to her lips that started sweet but escalated into hot when she opened her mouth and slid her tongue against his. She reached up, cupping the back of his neck, then she threaded her fingers through his thick, dark hair.

He scooped her up and placed her on the counter, spreading her legs. His erection pressed to her center, and she wrapped her legs around his hips, thankful for the ripped seam in the skirt that made it possible.

He raised his head and stared down at her, his eyes full of heat. "We're getting off topic. I was just going to kiss you and say I won't abandon you. You're stuck with me until we know what's going on." He then thrust his hips, his thick cock bumping against her clit and driving her wild as his mouth met hers again.

She didn't know this man, but he was just what she needed.

"Damn," he muttered against her mouth. "I need to taste you. Please will you let me taste you?"

She managed a breathy "Yes, please."

He dropped to his knees and widened the spread of her legs, positioning himself so her butt was on the counter and her legs were supported by his shoulders. His face was level with her center. He took a deep breath, then hooked a finger under the panel of her panties and tugged it to the side. He stared at her aching sex, then stroked her from vagina to clitoris with his tongue.

She groaned. He licked and sucked and explored, and pleasure swamped her. A delicious ache built as he focused on her clit, then slipped his tongue inside her as his thumb abraded her sensitive flesh.

This was wild, wanton, and wonderful, the way he devoured her in the kitchen. She was supposed to be cooking, not being pleasured by his tongue. But she gave herself over to the moment. No guilt. No hesitation. He was making her feel incredible, and she'd spent too much of her life working but not living.

And this? This was living.

His tongue returned to her clit. Hot, wet friction that drove her wild. He found her preferred rhythm and lapped at her like he was sprinting to her finish line. All at once, she came, a sharp, euphoric release. He pressed his tongue hard, holding her there, and the pleasure ratcheted higher. She rocked her hips against him, shouting and panting, unable to contain either the writhing or the sound.

His mouth left her center, and she opened her eyes to see him between her spread legs, his eyes hot and intense, his lips and beard slick with her wetness. She ran her thumb over the hair on his chin. "I need you inside me," she demanded. She was desperate for the feel of his hard length sliding deep. She also wanted him in her mouth with equal urgency. To explore every inch of his cock with her tongue, as he'd explored her.

She wanted to continue this raw, dirty, intense connection.

He smiled and shook his head. "No."

"Please? I'm not above begging."

He rose to his feet and undid the buttons on her top, exposing her plain beige bra. He pulled back a cup and sucked her nipple into his mouth. Her sex clenched and her hips bucked. He stroked her clit with his thumb as he slipped a finger inside her slick center. "You like that?" he whispered as he moved to free her other breast.

"I like *everything*. Now get inside me. Please."

His mouth found hers, and he kissed her as his fingers continued to play with her sex. "No, sweetheart. Because you promised me the world's best latkes. I'm not giving you my cock until after I've eaten everything on the menu."

He stepped back, leaving her panting on the countertop, breasts exposed, thighs spread, wet and ready for more attention.

"You are so damn sexy," he said. "With your prim pencil skirt slit to the upper thigh, demure blouse open, exposing your plump tits. And those black boots. I just want to stare at you. And lick you."

"And have sex with me?" she asked hopefully.

He laughed. "Oh yeah. And screw you blind."

"I put condoms in the cart when we were grabbing toiletries."

"I saw that."

"I know…it was presumptuous. But I thought it best to be prepared."

"I appreciate your forward thinking." He pulled up the cups of her bra but left the blouse unbuttoned and tucked into the waistband of her skirt, then lifted her from the counter and set her on her feet. "Ready to cook?" he asked.

She brushed her lips over his and said, "Almost." Then she slipped off her panties, pulling them over her boots, and dropped them on the floor. "There. Now I'm ready."

He laughed and hopped up on the counter she'd vacated. "Perfect. Mind if I watch?"

She handed him his glass of wine. "I was sort of counting on it."

She finished prepping the latkes and checked the brisket, which was reheating in the oven. She searched the cupboard and let out a squeal of delight at finding a cast iron skillet for frying the latkes.

Before heating the oil, she removed her silk blouse—anything she wore was likely to get spattered—and found an apron among the dish towels and table linens. It was a hideous thing—garish print fabric with overdone frills and ruffles—but it would protect her skin.

"You're killing my erection with that thing."

Her back would be to him as she faced the stove, so she twisted the skirt so the slit would expose the bottom curve of her left butt cheek.

"That's more like it," he said.

She set the oil to heating and took a sip of her wine, staring at the man who watched her with sexy, intense heat.

"Tell me about Christmas with your brother's family." She wanted to know everything about him. How had he so utterly captivated her on a day that should be one of the worst in her life?

And when had it happened? Was it during the kiss by the townhouse? Mt. Vernon's parking lot? Or had it happened in the Hanukkah aisle at Target?

"I've never spent Christmas with them before."

Guilt slithered up her spine. And she would likely keep him away this year too.

He shook his head, and she realized he could read her expression, giving her another question to ponder—when had she become so readable? Her last boyfriend's major complaint had been he couldn't read her. She kept her emotions too close and closed off.

But then, nothing quite like having your life cracked open to have all the emotions come spilling out.

"Not your fault, Leah. I'm choosing to stick with you. My call."

"But why?" she asked, even though she knew it was dangerous ground. The last thing she wanted was to talk him out of helping her.

"You said you were afraid, and I can do something about that. I want to be clear, helping you isn't about sex. I'd help you even if you turned me down cold and would want you even if you didn't need help. And if you decide you'd rather I sleep on the couch tonight, I'll still see this through with you." He held her gaze. "Make no mistake, I want you. Desperately. But that's not why we're here."

He glanced around the loaned cabin. "A few years ago, a friend told me he needed help, and I didn't believe him. Then, after that friend died, his sister showed up, and she said the same thing. And I didn't believe her either. I could have saved a bunch of people a lot of pain—including Chase—if I'd just listened to Vin the first time. Hell, maybe Vin would still be alive."

She noted the shadow of pain and regret in his eyes and crossed to stand before him. "You're a good man, Nate Sifuentes. Don't convince yourself otherwise." She kissed him softly. Closed mouth.

"I try." His hand cupped the back of her head. "And you are a fascinating woman." He kissed her hard. Deep. Changing the subject much as she had in the car when she'd asked him about Alaska. He released her and said, "Now, where are my latkes? It's almost one a.m., and I'm hungry."

She smiled and returned to the stove. She checked the oil's temperature by dipping her fingers in water and flicking them at the pan. It sizzled and spattered. Perfect. She quickly made two batches of latkes, draining them on paper towels when they were golden and crisp.

When the latkes were ready, she pulled the brisket from the oven and filled two plates with meat, potatoes, applesauce, and sour cream, while Nate set the table.

"If I kept kosher, the sour cream wouldn't be served on the same table with a meat dish," she explained as she removed the apron and donned her blouse again.

The menorah had long since burned out by the time they ate, so Nate lit a scented candle provided by the resort, and they ate by candlelight.

"These are, by far, the best latkes I've ever eaten," he announced halfway through the meal.

She rolled her eyes. "Also the only latkes?"

"That too, but damn. They're good."

She smiled. "Thank you. The brisket is a bit dry, but to be expected with premade."

"It's delicious. Thank you for sharing your Hanukkah with me."

She placed her hand over his and squeezed, not quite having the words for what this night meant to her. It was nothing short of a lifeline. She could be sleeping on the streets of DC tonight. She could be dead on the pavement by Mt. Vernon. Or be sitting in a jail cell in Arlington.

Done eating, they moved to the couch with their wine, facing the flickering light of the fire.

She leaned against him, and he wrapped an arm around her. She couldn't hold back her yawn as exhaustion settled in. The full belly and wine didn't help.

He kissed her temple. "It's okay if you want to sleep. It's been a long day, and it's after one. You need to rest."

She was conflicted. Exhaustion weighed her down, but still, she wanted—needed—to explore this crazy attraction to the fullest, seize the moment because, for all she knew, tomorrow would be even worse than today. Or rather, today would be worse than yesterday. She rubbed her eyes and said, "How about we sit in the hot tub for a bit?"

"You sure you want to?"

"Hot tubs are one of my favorite things in the world."

"Okay, then. I'll take the cover off while you strip."

Minutes later, she wrapped a thick towel around her naked body and stepped onto the rear deck. Sharp, frigid air hit her skin. Snow had been cleared from the deck, but the boards were slick and cold under her bare feet. The outside thermometer indicated it was twenty-five degrees. The cloudless night gifted them with thousands—millions—of twinkling lights, the Milky Way a thick swath without light pollution to hide it from view.

The cold air and bright sky invigorated her, and she faced Nate and dropped the towel on the deck. Goose bumps pebbled her skin, but she had the heat in his gaze to warm her.

"You're so damn beautiful," he said.

She liked the way he couldn't compliment her without even a mild expletive. Like she made him feel with extra intensity. He did the same to her.

"Get naked," she said.

"Yes, ma'am."

She scooped up her discarded towel and hung it on a hook by the tub, then climbed the steps and dipped a foot in the hot water, the liquid heat sharper and more delicious in contrast to her chilled skin on the cold, cold night. She sank into the warm water and hummed with pleasure.

Nate slipped inside the cabin, returning a minute later wearing nothing but a towel low around his hips. She grinned and went to the edge of the tub, then rested her chin on her hands, awaiting his big reveal.

His torso was a masterpiece. Broad shoulders, corded muscle along his arms, thick pecs, and a glorious six-pack capped a perfect V of musculature that arrowed downward under the towel.

A large tattoo graced his ribs, wrapping from front to back. Noticing her interest, he turned and raised his arm so his side was visible in the light that spilled from the bedroom.

"A hawk?" she asked at seeing the spread wings. Graceful lines in shades of black and gray created a web of feathers both fierce and delicate. It was stark, evocative, and magnificent.

"Yes. Hawk was my nickname on my Green Beret team. When I started working for Raptor, it felt like fate or something."

"It's beautiful," she said.

"Thank you." He grinned and dropped the towel.

She couldn't help but purr. Damn, but the cold was not an issue here. "*You're* beautiful," she added.

His grin widened as he climbed into the tub. He planted a fierce kiss on her lips, then said, "Thank you," again.

She hit the button for the jets, then settled onto a seat beside him. She closed her eyes and leaned back, allowing the water to massage her shoulders. "Please don't let me wake up from this. I'm having the sexiest, hottest, most wonderful dream."

He chuckled. "Me too."

The warmth of the water and the sound of the bubbles was a cocoon that made the world beyond the deck seem impossible. In the sky above, she could see a universe of stars that seemed more real than the darkness beyond the trees that surrounded the cabin. They sat there for several minutes, Nate's fingers massaging her neck and shoulders as they both gazed up at the glorious winter sky.

A satellite crossed the heavens, reminding her of the NASA dreams she'd had as a child. She brushed aside the thought. She could indulge in regret tomorrow. Right now, she was with a beautiful man who'd saved her life at least once today.

She rose from her seat and straddled Nate, facing him. She wrapped her arms around his neck and kissed him. "I want to forget everything and enjoy this. I want the rest of the world to not matter."

"Tonight, it doesn't. I can't make any promises about tomorrow."

"Then make love to me tonight."

He hit the button to turn off the jets, then wrapped his arms around her and rose from the water, lifting her. The cold air hit her skin, and she clung to him as he climbed from the tub, carrying her as if she were no burden, but she was no petite waif. She was a solid woman with curves.

His footing was sure on the slippery deck. Inside

the bedroom, he set her on the bed and stood above her, looking down, his gaze raking her body.

He was achingly, breathtakingly beautiful. Sculpted muscles. The artistry of the hawk tattoo. His erection, thick and perfect.

She reached for him, wrapping her hand around his cock and stroking from base to tip and down again. He groaned. She released him and scooted to the edge of the bed, then opened her mouth, inviting him inside.

He moved closer and traced her lips with the head, then pulled back before she could do more than kiss the tip. She leaned forward and managed to lick him, then leaned back, mouth open, desperate for him to take her mouth.

He teased her, thrusting the head between her lips, then pulling back before she could suck.

"This is not how blow jobs work," she said as she wrapped her hand around him. "*I'm* supposed to tease *you*."

"New rule. All teasing is done by me. Always. I've never seen anything more beautiful than your mouth begging for my cock. I intend to enjoy it."

"You think this is fun, wait until you feel my tongue on you as I suck."

He groaned and thrust into her mouth, and she had what she wanted. She sucked on the head and took him deep into the back of her throat. The hand wrapped around the base stroked as her other hand cupped his balls. She closed her eyes, pleasure drenching her as she had her way with him, loving the sound of his groans and pants as his hips jerked involuntarily because she was making him feel so desperately good.

She loved this, the slick feel of him in her mouth. The power of making him lose control as she sucked and stroked, coaxing him closer and closer to orgasm as his erection grew ever thicker, stretching her lips to open wider, filling her mouth until she could take no more.

His fingers found her vulva, and he spread her lips as he stroked her clit and slid fingers inside her. Pleasure saturated her as her mouth and vagina both received attention. Her sex was swollen with need, and she groaned even as she licked him.

She could feel his erection building and sucked harder in anticipation of swallowing his cum. All at once, he pulled from her mouth and spread her legs. "I want to be inside you."

"Hurry," she said.

He left her to grab a condom from the shopping bag and returned with the packet in his hand. He ran his cock over her center, teasing her clit and vagina as he'd teased her mouth, then he rolled the condom on and positioned himself between her thighs. He paused for a moment, then, with one sure thrust, he was inside her, expanding her. And it was crazy glorious, the thick feel of him.

"You are so beautiful," he said as he moved inside her. Hard, hot thrusts that triggered spasms of pleasure as he hit her G-spot. With each motion her pleasure built, higher, more intense than the kitchen-counter orgasm he'd given her earlier.

So intense, she couldn't contain a shriek. She covered her mouth, shocked by both the volume and decibel he'd elicited from her.

"Sweetheart, no one can hear us. We've got acres of woods to ourselves. Scream. Moan. Let me hear everything I'm doing to you."

And she did. She gave full voice to the orgasm that rocked her. Loud. Wild. Animal. She clawed at the sheets when the feeling became too intense, sliding up the bed toward the headboard.

He followed, his thick cock filling and stroking and giving no quarter. Pleasure jolted her with every hard thrust, and just when she thought she couldn't go higher, she broke, reaching the pinnacle. The sound she made was part groan, part yell, and he made a similar sound as he came just as hard, just as furious.

He collapsed on her, panting, and slowly she came down from the rush of the powerful, wild, intense orgasm.

"Damn," she whispered. "You're good at this sex thing."

He laughed. His lips nuzzled her neck as he said, "So are you." Then he turned and faced the ceiling, still breathing heavily. "That was... I mentioned it's been a long time for me, right?"

"Nearly two years."

"Yeah. I mean, I jack off regularly. But it's been that long since I've been with a partner and…as soon as I can move again, I need to get this condom off before it breaks, because damn, that was overdue."

He slowly rolled from the bed, and she watched his ass as he retreated to the bathroom. The wing of the hawk dipped down across his spine and touched the small of his back. She wanted to trace all of it with her tongue.

After he returned, she took her turn in the bathroom, then crawled into bed beside him. She noted that he'd covered the hot tub and closed the sliding glass door. The top of the bedding was damp thanks to their wet bodies after sitting in the tub, but it didn't matter as she snuggled against him.

Suddenly, her eyes were heavy with exhaustion. The intense day capped with hot sex had caught up with her. She tried to tell him how much she appreciated his help and how good he'd made her feel, but she suspected the words were an incoherent mumble.

He kissed her temple. "I'm going to protect you, Leah. I promise. Now sleep."

If he said more after that, she didn't hear it.

$\mathcal{N}$ate prowled the living room and kitchen of the cabin, unable to sleep. He couldn't figure out if he should feel guilty or not for having sex with Leah. She wasn't a Raptor client, but she was in a vulnerable position. He'd been careful. In every instance, she'd either initiated or had taken what had been meant to be a light kiss to the next level.

She'd put the condoms in the shopping cart, but he was the one who'd paid and rolled one on, when he knew damn well her life had fallen apart. But she was an adult woman who made her own decisions. He wasn't the kind of asshole to think he knew what was best for her. And she'd wanted the escape of pleasure he was more than eager to give her.

But was he simply justifying screwing her brains out because he'd wanted her so much that putting on the brakes hadn't crossed his mind in the heat of the moment?

And then there was the simple fact that she might not be the innocent woman she appeared to be. What if she was in some sort of conspiracy up to her eyeballs, and he'd just whisked her away to safety?

He didn't believe it—he'd never have slept with her if he did—but it would be sloppy of him to dismiss the possibility without more information.

He believed her, but to be good at his job, he had to leave the door open for doubt.

But damn, being inside her, hell, just being *near* her, made him feel all sorts of crazy things, have all sorts of ideas.

He'd told her the truth about his past relationships. In his first four years in Alaska, he'd had a lot of one-night stands along with a few friends-with-benefits arrangements. So many that they didn't appeal to him anymore. Now he wanted chemistry, combustion when it came to sex, but what happened between Leah and him was full-on flash fire.

He didn't think it was due to his long dry spell. It was one hundred percent Leah Ellis.

But he didn't have a damn clue how he was going to keep his promise to protect her when he knew nothing about what was going on. He couldn't even really question her because she couldn't violate her security clearance, and as a former Special Forces solider, he had to respect that.

He could ask her about Hathaway-Hollis, but it was hard to see how the toy drone company could be the issue here. But then, the company had a major promotional event scheduled for Christmas Day. The marketing campaign had led to thousands —hell, for all he knew, *millions*—of drone sales. As far as sales strategies went, it had been a brilliant success.

The product was slick, pretty, and environmental. Made of an aluminum alloy, not plastic, the drones were constructed from recycled material that was slightly heavier than the average toy drone and therefore required a more powerful motor. But that wasn't close to being the main selling point when it came to the shiny metallic toys.

The drones were billed as "peacemakers" and had AI technology that would trigger them to "befriend" other HH drones they met in the air. According to the ads, when two drones met, they would circle each other, then do a dance of friendship before zipping back to their owners who held their control wands.

The demos he'd seen of the AI was amazing, and he wondered if Leah was the brains behind the programming. If so, it wasn't surprising the military had wanted to test the technology. Drones that worked seamlessly in tandem, sharing data and navigating with minimal human interface, could be a wartime game changer.

The drones had been for sale for about a month now, but only a few had come out to play—making friends and appearing in Facebook and Instagram videos. The vast majority were hidden in closets, under beds, or already wrapped and under the tree. Whether the drone was already out and making peace with the neighbors or would be opened on Christmas Day, the company had found a way to keep the excitement going.

Nate grabbed his phone and opened the HH website to scan the list of parks where there would be a friendship festival at noon Pacific, three o'clock Eastern time on Christmas Day. If the turnout was anything close to what was expected, it would live up to its billing as the world's largest aeronautical show.

The whole thing was fueled by kids who'd begged their parents for an HH Peacemaker drone so they could show up at a park and watch it perform in the show. Sure, kids without drones could watch, but wouldn't it be more fun if they were participants?

If the Christmas Day events were successful, other drone Peace Gatherings would be scheduled, but in the meantime, given the massive sales, any time a kid showed up at the park with a drone, there was a good chance it would find a friend and make peace with the neighbors.

It was brilliant marketing, but also a little weird in that the kids wouldn't actually *fly* the drones in the Christmas Day show. The drones would fly themselves.

And Nate had to admit, he'd kind of like to see a hundred drones perform a spontaneous, synchronized dance. Apparently, the dance of the drones would be determined by the number of drones at the event, and releasing a new one partway through the routine would have a kaleidoscope effect, making the choreography shift and mirror and change the dance.

Was the woman he'd just made love to the brains behind the drone AI?

He should maybe feel intimidated at that thought, but mostly he was turned on. Literally, considering his cock was thickening as he remembered her body, how she'd responded to his touch. How she'd screamed her release, unable to contain her reaction to the power of the orgasm he'd given her.

Hands down the best sex of his life. And, he hoped, they were just getting started.

*L*eah woke with a start and checked the clock. Five a.m. Nate lay sleeping in the bed beside her. She had a fuzzy memory of him crawling into bed sometime in the dead of night, but maybe she'd imagined it.

The room was pitch-dark, but she could feel him next to her, hear his breathing, and wanted to savor this quiet hour with the man who'd started off as a driver but somehow become her rescuer and protector. Was this thing between them real or nothing more than timing and lust?

She liked him for real. She *wanted* this to be something. Even suspected he felt the same way. It was crazy. They hadn't even known each other twenty-four hours yet.

But she trusted her instincts. She was forty-three years old and single. She knew the game. She knew who was worth one night, who was worth dating, and when to bolt before the appetizers were delivered.

Nate Sifuentes was an order-dessert-and-take-him-home-and-eat-it-off-his-chest sort of guy.

Right now, she wanted to curl up against him and go back to sleep, but her subconscious had yanked her awake, demanding she start looking for reasons she'd been fired.

She slipped from the bed, moving carefully so as not to disturb Nate, and grabbed the Target bag from the floor. She'd slept in the nude and hadn't taken time to unpack last night.

In the living room, she sorted through the clothes and yanked off tags, then donned underwear, yoga pants, and a sweatshirt. She then dug through the bag and found one of the three prepaid phones they'd purchased along with cards to load up on data. They hadn't been sure which provider would have the best coverage in the area, so Nate had bought them all. Odds were coverage would still be lousy this close to Shenandoah, but at least they had slow Wi-Fi to work with.

She plugged in the phone and powered it on, entering the code from a data refill card. It took several minutes, but finally she had internet and went straight to a DC-area news site and looked for reports of a house fire in Arlington.

The story topped the headlines. Her stomach dropped at reading the lede. A woman of unknown age and identity had been found in the burned wreckage of the HH townhouse.

Chapter Six

$\mathcal{N}$ate woke to the sound of the car alarm. Not the loud kind that indicated someone had walked too close to a vehicle and annoyed everyone in a five-block radius. No, this was the alarm on his phone that let him know someone—who definitely wasn't him—was trying to drive his Raptor SUV without permission.

Bless Raptor and the company's ever-present paranoia that had them commission prox keys with thumbprint authorization. Leah hadn't seen him press his thumb to the back of the key last night when she drove, because the key had been in his pocket.

He slid from the bed and pulled sweatpants on over his boxer briefs and jammed his phone into a pocket, then crossed to the front door. He stepped onto the porch, barefoot and shirtless on the cold morning.

The soft light of predawn painted the snow in shades of dark gray. The sky had clouded over and threatened to snow. Cold wind ripped at his skin, but he barely noticed as he crossed his arms and stared at the woman he'd made love to just hours ago. She was behind the wheel of the SUV, desperately trying to put the engine in Drive so she could strand him on a mountain twenty miles from nowhere.

*L*eah pounded on the dashboard in a panic. Why wouldn't the damn car move? She needed to get the hell away from here. Away from Nate. Before her nightmare became his.

She looked at the dash. The engine was on but wouldn't shift into Drive, no matter how many times she moved the lever.

She glanced up—the windshield clear of frost because the air-flow system worked—and saw Nate cross his arms over his bare chest as he stared at her, his handsome face a hard mask of anger.

He stood in the gray light wearing only the sweatpants he'd purchased last night. He had to be freezing, but he didn't shiver or twitch. His stance showed just how huge he was, those muscular arms and thick pecs. The hawk tattoo was visible on his ribs, wrapping around his side, and her heart stuttered at the beauty of him while squeezing at the utter coldness of his expression.

She had to get out of here. Away from him. This thing between them couldn't go anywhere anyway. Best to leave while he was furious. Let him see this as betrayal. Let him believe the worst.

She hit the door lock button. Maybe that was the trick to getting the car into Drive or Reverse. Any direction that moved the wheels. Anything that could get her off this damn mountain.

But nothing happened, and now she felt tears forming. Worse, Nate stepped off the porch and stalked toward her, anger in each step.

She wiped at her eyes, willing the damn tears away as he came ever closer.

No. No. No. No!

Nate wouldn't be stranded. He had food and a phone, and Chase knew where he was and would arrive tomorrow night, if not sooner once Nate reached out to him. He'd get his SUV back. She'd leave it parked in front of her bank in Philly. Hell, she'd leave a suitcase full of cash in the front seat, payment for services rendered.

She didn't know what the hell was going on, but she was certain it wasn't about the military contract anymore. Not after seeing the headline. Not after reading the email.

She kept her gaze straight forward as Nate planted himself beside the driver's window. She wouldn't look at him. She'd figure out the secret to getting the car to move and drive away.

"Unlock the damn door, Leah."

Hoo boy. His tone was even angrier than his expression. She closed her eyes and felt tears burn.

Why couldn't she have met Nate a week ago, before her life went to hell?

He was everything she hadn't known she wanted. Her relationship résumé included over twenty years of dating experience. She'd done the club scene in her early twenties and had tried online dating before any of the major sites were a household name. She'd dated coworkers—before establishing a personal rule never to date a coworker again—and had swiped in every direction imaginable.

In all those years, she'd had good dates and awful ones. Good sex and awful sex. She'd kissed a lot of toads and even a few princes, but she couldn't remember ever feeling about a man the way she did about Nate after just a few hours. Hell, she'd had this fluttery feeling even before they'd had sex.

And after sex?

Her feelings only burned stronger.

But the timing was wrong and she couldn't have him, couldn't have any kind of fantasy that ended with her life not being utterly destroyed. She'd worried about being set up for treason, but now it looked like she could face murder charges.

And Nate could be the next victim.

Chapter Seven

Nate pounded on the window again. "Unlock. The goddamn. Door." His anger was reaching new levels as she continued to avoid his gaze, and he had to take a deep breath to steady himself. He didn't want to scare her. But he was livid.

How could she do this after last night?

She tried again to put the car in Reverse, then slammed her hand on the steering wheel.

"Leah. It won't go into Drive. The engine is locked. You aren't going anywhere, so open the damn door."

He stood barefoot in the snow, too angry to feel the pain in his feet. Part of him, somewhere, suspected it wasn't anger he was feeling, but he didn't want to face the real emotion her attempt to flee had triggered.

Her forehead hit the steering wheel and her

body shook. He locked down his emotions tight. He couldn't be swayed by tears. He needed answers, dammit.

He'd protected her and risked his job for her. He'd given her his body. His friend had given her a safe place to stay.

And she was trying to steal his company car and run away.

"You realize stealing the SUV would get me fired, right? My standing with the company is on thin ice as it is, and you'd screw me over this way?"

She raised her head and looked at him, tears streaking down her face. She swiped at them, but more fell.

It was the unstoppable tears and devastation on her face that shattered the shell of anger he'd wrapped himself in when the phone woke him with the alarm. He could see the terror in her eyes just as he had last night at Mt. Vernon.

Okay, so maybe she hadn't been planning to screw him and run. Which meant something must have happened.

With his anger obliterated, he felt the burn of cold against his feet. The wind on his skin caused him to shiver, and it took him a moment to realize the flakes that swirled in the air hadn't been blown off tree branches with each cold gust. Snow was beginning to fall.

He couldn't stand out here arguing with her much longer. He'd wanted to give her a chance to open the door on her own, but she'd given him no choice. He pulled out his phone and unlocked the car, then yanked open the door before she realized what was happening.

"Dammit, Leah. Don't force me to be the asshole here. Get in the cabin now."

Her eyes had gone wide with shock. He reached across her, unbuckled her seat belt, and grabbed the SUV's prox key from the center console—careful not to touch his thumb to the reader on the back. He hit the button to turn off the engine and grabbed the shopping bag full of clothes from the passenger seat, then stepped back so she could descend from the seat under her own power.

He wouldn't touch her or in any way physically force her to do anything.

He turned and marched for the cabin door, pebbles of ice biting into his feet with each step. Behind him, he heard the car door close and footsteps crunch in the snow.

He entered the cabin without looking back and stalked to the bedroom, tossing the bag of clothes on the bed where he'd made love to her.

He closed his eyes, swamped by memories. He could still feel her hands on his body. Tracing the hawk tattoo. Her mouth on him. He could hear the sounds she'd made as he'd come inside her.

She didn't owe him anything. Sex was sex. Given and received freely. They'd made no commitments, offered no foolish words of feelings they couldn't possibly have in such a short acquaintance. But still, her attempt to flee—and rob him and get him fired—was a kick in the balls.

The first woman he'd wanted to bang in two years. He'd learned to ignore the simple sexual itch that needed scratching. What he'd felt for Leah sure as hell hadn't been that. But damn, he should have stuck with one-night stands, because adding any sort of emotion to the equation was asking for trouble.

Nate should have accepted he was a loner when he stopped wanting sex for sex's sake. He should have invested in a Fleshlight and called it a day.

Why had he believed that if he moved to the DC area and had more options, he might find someone who could be more than just an itch scratcher? How had he convinced himself that he was not just worthy of love, but also capable of it?

His skin burned from standing in the cold too long. He crossed to the bathroom and locked the door. The lock was flimsy, and she'd easily break in, so he put the phone and car key on the shelf next to the shower. If she entered while he bathed, he'd be able to grab them.

He stepped into the shower, turning his face to the hot spray. His emotions were shot to hell. He wasn't the operator he'd spent the last eight years training others to be, nor was he the soldier he'd been for the last twenty-plus years.

Somehow, someway, Leah Ellis had managed to rip out his heart in eighteen short hours.

*L*eah paced the living room, dreading facing Nate but knowing it was inevitable. It was either face him or freeze in the snow.

She'd screwed up, but she wouldn't compound it by risking her life and trying to hike her way out of this mess, much as she wanted to.

His shower was brief, and he stepped into the living room with damp hair, again wearing only the sweatpants he'd had on earlier.

The hawk tattoo was even more magnificent in full light. His body all the more impressive. And she'd had him. All of him. Her special gift on the first night of Hanukkah.

She'd managed to get her crying under control and washed her face in the kitchen sink. She met his gaze now, dry-eyed and composed. She would not let him know she was hurting. It served no purpose when she needed to push him away. She wouldn't let him get sucked into this ugly vortex that had nothing to do with him. He would survive and move on.

"I'm sorry," she said. "I appreciate all your help. But now I need to leave."

"The hell you do. I thought we were in this together."

"I can't help what you thought. This is my problem and mine alone."

"Why are you doing this?"

She gave him a defiant look. "Listen. You were just a screw. A really good one, but just a screw nonetheless. I shouldn't have taken advantage of you. For that, I'm sorry."

"Bull. Fucking. Shit."

She couldn't help herself, she laughed. He wasn't the most creative at cursing, but he said each word with gusto, infusing them with emotion they might otherwise lack.

Dammit. She was even turned on by the way he cursed.

"I need to go to Philadelphia."

"Why?"

"I can't tell you. Military secret."

"Bullshit. You're a crappy liar."

She happened to be an excellent liar. She just couldn't lie to *him*. Which was alarming. How did he learn to read her so well, so quickly?

"Listen, I'm sorry you got wrapped up in this, but that, at least, isn't my fault. I didn't hire you. But I can get you out of this. Take me to a train station, buy me a ticket to Philly, and you can be done with me. I'll pay you back as soon as I get to my bank and can withdraw money."

"You don't have ID."

"They have my fingerprints on file and they know my face. When your account has enough zeros, bankers pay attention."

"If you're so wealthy, why were you living in a house owned by HH?"

"It was a six-month temporary assignment. Why bother finding my own place when I could use the company townhouse?"

"Then why did you sell your place in Philly?"

It shouldn't surprise her he'd tracked down the real estate transaction. He'd been up in the middle of the night and had Raptor's access to information. Hell, he probably had her social security number, the name of her first pet, and the name of the street she'd lived on when she was ten years old.

"The house in Philly was my mom's dream home. I bought it for us to share when she retired. When she died, I didn't want to live in such a huge space by myself. It was too painful without her. I put it on the market in the summer once I was sure I'd end up relocating to DC for a while. It sold fast, and I ended up living in a short-term rental for a month while waiting for my security clearance to go through."

"How did your mother die?" His voice was soft. Sympathetic.

"She had a heart attack. I came home from work one day, and she was…gone. She was only sixty-eight. She'd retired a year before and moved in with me to enjoy her golden years. It wasn't supposed to go that way." She swiped at the tears that always fell when she faced the suddenness of her mom's passing. "She was supposed to have at least twenty years to enjoy retirement and nag me for grandchildren." Given that Leah was in her early forties, it was highly unlikely those grandchildren would ever exist, but still, she touched her belly as she always did at the thought, knowing that if she ever did have a baby or decided to adopt, her child would never know the love of the only person who had ever loved Leah unconditionally. She swiped at another tear. "It was just me and my mom for a lot of years. We were really close."

Nate crossed the small space that separated them. He cupped her face in his big palm, his thumb brushing at the tears that wouldn't stop flowing. "I'm sorry."

In the year since her mother had died, no one had hugged her to offer comfort for her grief. It was her own fault. She didn't have friends outside work and kept her coworkers at a distance. It would have felt odd to receive a hug from Ainsley even though they were friends. And it definitely would have felt weird if Tim Hathaway or Michelle Hollis had tried to hug her.

Dex, of course, had offered a different kind of comfort. And there was nothing soothing to be found in the power play.

So now here she was, a year after her mother's death, and Nate Sifuentes was the first person to offer her true comfort in her grief, and he also happened to be the only man who had given her physical pleasure in far too long.

She leaned into him and brushed her lips over his. She wanted to take the comfort he offered. She wanted more physical pleasure. She wanted to feel less alone and more cherished.

Her tongue slipped between his lips. He let her in, and his tongue stroked hers. She melted into him. She needed this—him—so much.

His hand moved from her face to cup the back of her head. The kiss was deep and hot, and her worries evaporated.

Then he abruptly raised his head and pushed away from her. "What the hell? No. You aren't going to distract me with sex."

Her body had flushed with heat as the kiss intensified, and now she went cold, as if she'd just been tossed in the snow.

"I wasn't—"

"Right. Listen, I might not be a technical super-genius like you, but I'm not stupid. You've been using my attraction to you from the start—from unbuttoning your blouse the moment you climbed into the back of my car to stealing my wallet to screwing me so I wouldn't pay attention to where I left the damn car keys. No more."

She *had* played the stupid game with the button and flirted with him to get to his wallet. But that he believed the sex had been a ploy bothered her. She hadn't been playing games then, and it pissed her off that he couldn't see it. "I didn't sleep with you so I could steal the keys."

"Yeah, well, that's how it looks from my perspective."

She took two steps backward, then turned and paced the small living room. "I'm sorry—"

"You said that already. It's feeling pretty meaningless at this point."

"What do you want from me?"

"Something real would be a nice start."

She took a deep breath. "I'm scared."

"You played that card already."

Her anger spiked. "I am! Dammit! I'm terrified because a dead body was found in my apartment. A woman died in the fire. Someone is trying to frame me for murder, and I got an email that implied you're next on the hit list."

Chapter Eight

$\mathcal{N}$ate stared at Leah, not as shocked by her words as he should be. He'd guessed something must have happened. What he didn't get was why she'd choose to run instead of telling him what was going on.

"What are you involved in, Leah?"

"I don't know." She rubbed a hand over her face. "I got an email saying Ainsley's missing."

"Who is Ainsley?"

"Ainsley Weisz is the head of marketing at HH. The Christmas Day events were her brainchild. I was head of AI engineering for Peacemaker. The product wouldn't be possible without me, but Ainsley is the one who found a way to sell it to two million American families."

"Two million?" Holy crap. That was a lot of drones.

"Give or take. Those were the numbers as of

Friday. Our manufacturer in China wasn't able to keep up with demand. Thanks to Ainsley, who, according to an anonymous email, is missing."

"Let me see this email."

She pulled one of the prepaid cell phones he'd purchased last night from her coat pocket, and turned it on. "It's a free online account I use when I can't access my work email. I rarely use it, and only a handful of people have it—coworkers, a few friends from my Silicon Valley days. No one connected to the military contract has this address, so this can't be related to the government job."

After the phone restarted, she opened her email and handed him the phone.

He noted the time stamp. The email had been sent just over an hour before.

Whore. Bitch. Slut. Did you plan this with the Raptor guy? Are you feeding him government secrets? Is that why you were fired? Your innocent act won't hold up. Ainsley is missing. Was she helping you sell military secrets to mercenaries? I will find you, traitor. I will stop you. I will stop him.

He checked the sender information. It was a random series of numbers and letters from another free online email provider.

"The only person who knows of Raptor's—*my* —involvement with you is the person who followed us last night. A search on the SUV license plate would show Raptor as the registered owner. That's the only way they would know. Freddy sure wouldn't tell HH he was sending in a pinch hitter."

"I know." She stopped pacing and stood in front of him. "Ainsley was a friend. I'm worried about her. And if she died in the fire, I'm terrified I'll be a suspect, and doesn't that make me a shitty friend, to be worried about myself?" She resumed pacing, her hands cupped over her nose and mouth, as if in prayer. "If the person who sent that email is the person who followed us last night, then they've already tried to kill me once. And they threaten me in the email."

"I promised I would protect you, Leah."

"I know. That's not why I tried to run. It's the second part. The 'I will stop him' line. That's a threat to you. I was trying to get away from you. To protect you."

Nate stared at her and tried to shove his ego aside to figure out what this all meant. He needed to get his head out of his ass and think. "Why didn't you wake me? Why run?"

"Why hesitate? Why stay?" she countered. "The email had been sent only a few minutes before. If it contained a Trojan that could snatch GPS data, the sender could know where we are. I wanted to lead him away from you. ASAP."

Nate pulled off the back of the phone and yanked the battery. "Does it have a Trojan?"

"I don't know. I didn't waste time by cracking

open the email. If I had a VPN set up, I would, but…" She held up her hands, indicating the cozy, low-tech cabin with weak Wi-Fi and limited cell service.

"Okay, first thing we need to do is call the police in Arlington and share everything you know. I was going to suggest we do that this morning anyway. We should have made the call last night, but it was clear you needed a break, and the difference between one in the morning and now—after all, I didn't know a woman was inside the townhouse—didn't seem important."

He slipped an arm around her, pulling her to him. "You have an alibi. Three alibis including Chase and Josh. Plus, you're caught on camera at the Navy Yard coming and going. It would be damn hard to pin a murder on you when we can show you hadn't been in the townhouse since you left for work at…what time?"

"Nine. I slept in because I was up until two working on the fix for HH."

"We can handle this, Leah. First thing to do is get you a lawyer. You just said you have money, so that's not an issue. I thought rich people knew about lawyering up from the get-go."

She pursed her lips, but then she gave him a faint smile. "I haven't always been rich. That's sort of new, and I tend to forget because I'm always working."

"You're an ace programmer, forty-three years

old, and only newly rich? What's wrong with you? I thought all computer geniuses made their first million by twenty-seven and billion by thirty-five."

"I'm a late bloomer."

"Well, good thing I like late bloomers." He ran his fingertips along her forehead and temple and asked her the one question he shouldn't. "Did you mean it when you said I was just a screw?"

"No."

"Good." He lowered his head and brushed his lips over hers. "Don't ever try to bolt like that again. Have faith in me. I work in private security. I'm not afraid of a pathetic emailed threat."

"What if whoever sent that email knows where we are now?"

"Then they can reveal themselves by showing up at our door. I'm sure the police will have a lot of questions for them, starting with why they came after you last night."

She closed her eyes and took a deep breath. "It was really dumb of me to try to run, wasn't it?"

"Not dumb. Panic. Which is what they wanted. You weren't thinking straight. You had a stressful day and little sleep."

"You forgive me?"

He tucked her hair behind an ear. "Of course."

She rose on her toes and pressed her mouth to his. She whispered, "Show me. Make me feel forgiven," then slipped her tongue between his lips.

He let her in, sucked on her tongue, and as if a

switch had been flipped, he was all in, scooping her up in his arms and pressing her against the wall, her plea for forgiveness all the incentive he needed.

She wrapped her legs around his hips. He kissed her hard and deep as his erection pressed against her hot center.

He'd said he wanted spark, and Leah was a torrent of flame. He was hot and thick and wanted to make her feel wild but also cherished. Wanted to make love to her and take her fast and hard at the same time.

"I need you inside me, Nate." She panted and gripped his shoulders, rocking her hips so his cock would press her clit.

Multiple layers of clothing separated their bodies; that had to change. He carried her to the couch and set her on her feet in front of it, then dipped a hand under the waistband of her yoga pants and slid his fingers into her soft, wet folds. She jolted with pleasure.

He chuckled as his ego soared. "You get that wet just for me?"

She rocked into his hand. "Yes. Your cock. Your mouth. Your fingers. You make me so hot, I'm burning up."

He yanked down the pants and dropped to his knees, putting his mouth on her even as his hands pulled off her tennis shoes and socks and then tugged the tight cloth first over one foot, then the other. She placed her hands on his shoulders for balance, and he spread her legs and licked her.

She pulled the long-sleeve T-shirt over her head and unclasped her bra as he stroked her with his tongue. He looked upward to see her cupping and massaging her full breasts as she panted and gasped at the pleasure he was giving her.

She was a woman in her forties, evidenced by the few strands of gray that streaked her hair and her soft, lush curves. She knew her body and her pleasure, and that was hot beyond belief.

She released her breasts and threaded her fingers through his hair. He lifted one of her legs and pulled it over his shoulder, opening her legs wider so she straddled his face. His tongue slid inside her vagina, and she made a guttural sound that drove him wild.

His tongue returned to her clit, his beard abrading the insides of her thighs. She tightened her grip on his hair, hovering on the brink of orgasm. He could feel the tension in her inner thighs and hear it in the shift in her breathing.

"Please, Nate, I want you inside me when I come. I need you, Nate. Now." Her panting grew harder, more desperate. "Please. Please. Please."

"Come for me. The condoms are in the bedroom."

"Get them. Please. Please."

He licked her clit again, then slipped his shoulder from beneath her leg and stood. "Don't move." He darted for the bedroom. Condom in hand, he returned to the living room and stripped off the sweatpants and briefs.

She wrapped her hand around his thick erection and stroked him, then dropped to her knees and took him in her mouth, and it was his turn to let out a guttural groan. She placed a hand on his hip and nudged him around, sucking even as she positioned him in front of the couch. He lowered onto the cushions and she knelt before him, her lush body between his knees as she took his cock deep into her throat, one hand stroking the shaft while the other cupped his balls.

He threaded his fingers through her hair, and she met and held his gaze. There were few things that were sexier than eye contact with Leah while she sucked his cock.

He was so close to coming, but he wanted what she'd begged for—to come inside her as she came too. He ripped open the condom packet and said, "Sit on my cock."

She smiled and took the condom. She released him from her mouth and unrolled the latex sheath down his hard shaft. In one smooth movement, she climbed on his lap and sank down on him, taking him deep.

She kissed him as she moved her thighs, rising then sinking down on him again and again. His hands on her ass lifted and lowered her even as he rocked his hips, using the spring of the couch to thrust upward, penetrating her with hard, fast strokes.

He moved one hand between their bodies and thumbed her clit. As if he'd pressed a magic button, she released his mouth from a deep kiss and let out a sharp yell, arching her back and clenching tight around his cock. He kept up the pressure on her clit and thrust upward, his own release coming in a rush after the intense buildup.

She continued coming as his orgasm faded, so he continued stroking her clit and she clenched on him again, triggering another burst of pleasure before she collapsed on him, breathing heavy, all soft limbs and satisfaction.

He held her that way for a long moment, still inside her. Replete. He trailed kisses along her neck and breathed in the scent of her.

She shifted, and he slipped from her body. He should get up and take care of the condom but didn't want to move. Spotting the boxer briefs on the arm of the couch, he decided to sacrifice them to the cause and wrapped the used condom in the cloth, then set them aside and shifted to lie down on the couch with Leah's body on top of his.

He'd loaded up the woodstove in the night, then turned down the airflow, and a few remaining embers still burned, giving the room a cozy glow as dawn began to break over their mountain hideaway.

He ran his fingers through her short hair and

stroked her cheek with his fingers. "The first moment I saw you, I was blown away. You walked out of that gate with your head held high in those kickass, sexy boots, and I was done for."

"And I took one look at you and knew you weren't just a driver."

"Hey, woman. My brother's a driver. He employs drivers. Drivers are people too." But he laughed. She wasn't *just* a passenger for him either.

She grinned. "You know what I mean." She ran her hands down his body. "Your body is a work of art. And I don't just mean the tattoo, but that's amazing too." She traced the ink on his ribs. "How did you get the nickname Hawk?"

"It's a little ridiculous."

"Try me."

"I have…an abnormally long reach." He wrapped his arms around her, partly as demonstration but mostly because he liked the way she felt in his arms. "And hawks have a long wingspan. One day, I was messing around during basic, arms stretched wide, and one of the guys says something about how I looked like a damn hawk circling for the kill, and considering how bad nicknames can get in the military, I went all in so it would stick. Lucky for me, it did, and I spent the next fourteen years being called Hawk more than any other name."

"Does anyone still call you that?"

"Here and there. The guys at the Alaska

compound picked it up, which is why Chase uses it sometimes—he worked there a few years ago. Moving here, it was more natural to go by Nate. My brother sure as hell never called me Hawk, and Isabel Dawson—Senator Ravissant's wife—is one of my few friends here, and she always called me Nate."

"You're friends with the senator's wife?"

"Yeah. I was close to her brother in the months before he died. I'm a connection to him."

Guilt stabbed at him. Vin had died in a training accident that Nate later found out was no accident at all. And if he'd just listened… Just paid attention… He could have stopped it.

Did he deserve these moments of happiness when he'd failed Vincent Dawson, who was one of the finest men he'd ever known? Vin didn't get to have moments like this, with a beautiful woman in his arms.

Vin had told Nate about the nightmares. And he hadn't listened. When Isabel showed up telling the same story, he figured the grieving woman was searching for someone to pin the blame on and had gotten wrapped up in Vin's delusions. If he'd taken Vin seriously, and later Isabel seriously, he could have saved a lot of people—like Chase—from suffering.

As he'd told Leah last night, that was why he'd acted when she said she was scared. He would never again ignore a person's pleas. Not when he was in a position to do something.

She traced the edges of the hawk feathers with her nails. "You don't like your job with Raptor, though, do you?"

"Yes and no. It's a good job, but I've never been a favorite of the home office. They don't trust me because Robert Beck hired me. I wasn't a Beck sycophant either, but it's not like they see that."

"So you don't like your boss."

"It's not that simple. I actually like Keith, I'm just bothered that I've been skipped over for promotion repeatedly, while people he or Rav hired leap past me in the company hierarchy. I'm not even saying the people they've promoted aren't good. It's just that I have more experience than all of them. Even Keith, the CEO."

"Have you filed a complaint with management or human resources?"

"No."

"You should. I can give you tips on how to frame it. One thing I know is how to deal with management." Her face reddened. "I mean, I did. Before yesterday."

He ran a finger over her lips. "I'm pretty sure yesterday is about something else entirely."

"Me too."

He turned his gaze to the ceiling. "I'm not a supergenius programmer. I don't have your leverage when it comes to management."

She kissed his chest. "And I'm a woman, the senior programmer who spearheaded the Peacemaker project, which has led to the biggest holiday sales for any toy drone manufacturer ever. We're the *it* toy this year. I'm at the top of my field—one in which men actively try to exclude women. I didn't get where I am because of my brains—there are plenty of women in tech who are smarter than me. It's because I learned how to navigate HR and management every time someone tried to slam a door in my face."

He kissed her temple. "That is so badass." He loved that she wasn't shy about her success. She didn't assume his ego couldn't handle being with a woman who was older, smarter, and richer than him. Maybe that was what had drawn him to her from the start. She'd carried herself like the powerful woman she was—even when fired and escorted through the gate. "Okay. I'll do it. I'll tell Keith I want a raise and better assignments."

She ran a hand over his ass. "I hate to mention it, but your negotiation position will probably be weakened thanks to your association with me."

"And if Keith doesn't see that you're being set up, he's not the man he's supposed to be. Josh will go to bat for you—he's Keith's best friend—and Chase is on Team Leah too."

"I have a team?"

"Hell yeah. I'm your head cheerleader."

She laughed, then tucked her head against his

chest and whispered, "I don't deserve you, Nate Sifuentes."

"No, what you don't deserve is what's happened to you in the last twenty-four hours." He kissed her cheek. "You know how to navigate in the business world, but private security and ops—that's my thing. We're going to figure out what's going on, starting with finding out who died in the townhouse and who sent you that email."

Chapter Nine

*L*eah hit the End button on the cell phone, then held it in her lap as they sped down the highway. "Arlington police isolated the Trojan. Frankly, I'm irritated that whoever sent the email didn't realize I'd suspect spyware. Do they not realize I'm head of the frigging coding team?"

"Well, they also screwed up in not considering you'd give the Arlington police access to your account."

She frowned. "I feel like such a fool. I was ready to run to Philly and question everyone in the company instead of talking to the police and letting them conduct the interviews. Thank you for stopping me."

"That email was designed to send you into a panic. It's hard to think in that situation. My whole job is to train people how to work through panic and chaos."

"This isn't combat, though."

"No, but the principle is the same. You felt the threat, and fight or flight kicked in."

"I chose flight."

"And my job is to teach people to fight."

She gazed out the window at the fresh snow. The morning storm had been light, and now, in the early afternoon, the roads were clear and dry as they headed to the nearest superstore to buy a laptop, another cell phone, and, if they could, a Hathaway-Hollis drone.

She'd spent hours this morning on the phone with investigators, telling everything she knew about the fire at the townhouse—which wasn't much considering she hadn't been inside—and explained that she'd left because after being nearly run down at Mt. Vernon, she feared for her life. Thankfully, she'd been able to give them the number of the police report filed by Josh, and Detective Brown confirmed other witnesses had reported the incident.

The email from the unknown sender raised more questions than it answered. It said nothing about the fire but claimed Ainsley was missing—a detail the police were looking into. If Ainsley was the woman who died in the fire, what had she been doing in the townhouse after the NSA had seized it? No one outside the NSA should have been allowed inside until it was cleared by officials.

The idea that Ainsley might be gone made

Leah's heart ache. She didn't have many friends—a hazard of being a workaholic—but Ainsley was a workaholic too, so their friendship had developed along lines that fit them both.

Twelve miles from their cabin hideaway, they reached the store, which was packed with people finishing up their holiday shopping. They made their way to the back, where the electronics department was located. Leah chose the best laptop they had in stock, and Nate put it on his credit card. "We also want to get one of those HH drones. You know the ones—the Peacemaker—"

"Sold our last one days ago," the saleswoman said. "We might get another shipment tomorrow, but you'd probably have to line up at five a.m. And we might not get any. Virginia Beach has been hogging the shipments, and the DC-area stores have gotten the rest."

She'd expected that response, but it had been worth a try. Plus, it gave her a little thrill knowing the thing she'd helped create was this year's sensation.

This week was supposed to be her finest hour.

As they grabbed more groceries, Nate said, "I'm sorry we couldn't get a drone."

She'd wanted the drone so she could test the Peacemaker protocol she'd uploaded at two a.m. on Sunday, but it wasn't vital. It was just one of the tests she'd planned to run this week with the half dozen drones she'd had in the HH townhouse.

She shrugged. "I guess it means I don't have a Christmas present for you now."

"I haven't gotten you a Hanukkah present either."

She patted the laptop. "You got me a very good present." She winked at him. The computer had cost nearly four thousand dollars, and she planned to transfer the money to him when they got back to the cabin.

He laughed. "Well then, aren't I the extremely generous new boyfriend?"

She cocked her head. "So, you're my boyfriend now?"

"Do you want to continue seeing each other once all this is over?"

"Yes." Absolutely. Maybe even desperately.

"Do you want to date anyone else?"

"No. And I don't share."

"Good. Me either. So yeah, based on those criteria, it sounds like we're officially a couple."

"Then I really need to find you a Christmas present. Or a Hanukkah present. Or whatever we decide to call it."

He wrapped an arm around her waist. "I just thought of something you can give me. It's like, one of my favorite things in the world. Doesn't cost a thing."

She brushed her lips over his. "I gave you that this morning already. And last night."

"Yeah, but isn't Hanukkah an eight-day event?"

She laughed. "This mixed-holiday relationship thing really is the best of all worlds, isn't it?"

"Yes. Yes, it is." He leaned down and whispered in her ear, "I'm really quite crazy about you, Leah Ellis."

Her body went all fluttery. Standing in the middle of a packed store with shoppers in a holiday frenzy shoving their way past on all sides, she was having a moment. Like a she-might-melt kind of moment. She found her voice. "I'm pretty crazy about you too, Hawk."

He grinned at her use of his nickname.

She leaned into him and whispered, "And by the way, Hawk might be the sexiest nickname ever."

"Let's get the rest of the things we need and get out of here."

They picked up more food—enough for a few days plus a leg of lamb for Christmas dinner—and condoms, and she managed to slip a few small puzzles and games in the cart that would serve as presents on Christmas Day.

Resupplied, they returned to the cozy cabin. As much as she wanted to relax and play and make love, now that she had a computer, she had work to do. She couldn't access the HH servers with this machine, but she knew of a few back doors she could exploit.

Nate took over cooking, and she planted herself in front of the keyboard. She was immersed in the work, oblivious to everything as she hacked the HH email system. She lost all track of time until Nate placed a hand on her shoulder. "It's almost thirty minutes after sunset."

Warmth flooded her at his reminder. She placed her hand over his and squeezed. "Thank you. I'd have missed it and then been so mad at myself."

He kissed her temple. "My pleasure."

Nate stood by her side again as she said the blessing, then lit the menorah and set it in the window. They sat together on the couch with glasses of wine, watching the candles burn. She leaned against him, feeling so damn comfortable, it defied logic. But she'd decided to lean in and enjoy.

After a while, he asked, "Have you found anything on the computer?"

"A lot of bureaucratic emails. Nothing about me or why I was fired yet. A few alarming emails about problems with Peacemaker and some questions about who would fix it now that I'm out of the picture. Naturally, Dex stepped up to the plate. He's wanted my job for three years now."

"Could that be what this is about? A coup?"

"Maybe, but I don't understand how Ainsley fits in. Or the fire. Or the car at Mt. Vernon. But I could totally see Dex doing something to make it look like I jeopardized national security to get me fired if he could."

"Tell me about Peacemaker. Given the timing, it feels like this must relate somehow."

"Peacemaker is the AI part of the drone. I—and my team, which includes Dex—finished the basic coding for it a year ago so we could roll it out for this holiday season. The events that are happening on Christmas Day are a special element—a specific Peacemaker dance that will only happen at three o'clock Eastern, noon Pacific on December twenty-fifth. That's the piece I had to fix last week because Dex screwed it up. Each dance will be unique—depending on the number of drones at each event—but there's a basic kaleidoscope pattern I created at the start. It will follow the laws of mirrors and flow into other patterns I set up. The flight is based on models developed to account for wind, velocity, battery life, and other variables."

"So, just when I think I've wrapped my brain around how smart you are, you say something like that and my mind is blown again. I never considered that you can't just write code like the kind that makes a computer or smartphone work. It has to work on a physical level with variables you can predict but can't control. And you need…every combination. Wind, rain, heat."

"Yes. But that's the beauty of algorithms. They do the heavy lifting."

"But you have to write the algorithm."

She nodded. "Yes. That part is me. And my team."

"So in two days, the big simultaneous Christmas

Day events, that's basically the pinnacle of everything you've been working on."

"Yes. I spent four years developing the AI and most of the last year refining it. When all those drones take flight at three on Wednesday, that will be because of *me*. The Peacemaker concept was Tim Hathaway and Michelle Hollis's idea, and they paid me the big bucks to make it work. Ainsley came up with the genius marketing plan, but no one would have anything to sell without me."

She closed her eyes, thinking of all the long hours. The arguments. The celebrations when they finally nailed it. "Dex would have been reduced to little more than blubbering ego two years ago. Michelle—she's got a strong programming background—knew it was beyond her ability, so she brought me in. The only other person in the company who might have the brains for it is Kevin Marks, but he's young and a bit too blinded by his own greatness to know when to listen to others and how to work with a team."

"Had you planned to go to one of the events?"

She nodded. "Wouldn't miss it." Then she frowned. "Except I guess I will."

"You don't have to miss it. We can go to one here or in the DC area. Which one had you planned to go to?"

"The one at the ballpark in DC. With the restrictions on flying drones in the district, it was hard to find a venue in the capital, so it's the one event that HH is actually sponsoring. We got special permission given the proximity to Reagan National Airport for the drones to fly no higher than three hundred and fifty feet for twenty minutes on the twenty-fifth as long as they stay within the boundary of Nationals Park. It cost HH a fortune to rent the stadium on Christmas Day for an open, nonticketed event."

"With sales through the roof, I have a feeling HH can afford it."

"Yeah. Ainsley really was a genius."

"You're using past tense."

"I feel sick at the possibility. She was my friend. *Is* my friend. God. I don't know what tense to use."

"How could she get into the townhouse?"

"She had a key. She used the townhouse when she traveled to the DC area—and she'd been there a lot to plan the stadium event. She'd asked if she could stay even when I was living there. Considering I'm barely there, I said sure. But she never stayed with me. I don't know if she came down and stayed in a hotel or not. I was too busy with the Navy Yard contract and fixing Dex's mess with Peacemaker."

"Could she have been planting evidence for the NSA to find?"

"She worked in marketing, so it's hard to imagine she'd have access to anything like that—or why she'd do it. We were friends."

"It's possible you aren't the target, but HH is.

It's a cutthroat business, and HH is the current leader. Maybe a competitor wanted to bring the company down before the big event that seals your place in the top spot."

"It would make sense to target Ainsley and me if that's the motive. She and I are the two prongs of the company's success this year. Her genius marketing, my coding. HH needs us both."

"But you were fired and she went missing right as both your jobs were essentially complete."

"Yes." She considered HH's competitors, many of whom had offered her jobs in the last two years, but even without a no-compete clause, Leah would have been loyal. She sat up straight. "A year ago, I fired a programmer who'd been working on Peacemaker. He was copying the code to either start his own company or take a job with a competitor."

"How did you find out what he was doing?"

"Actually, it was Ainsley who caught him. She was working late one night and saw my office light on. My mother had just died, and she was surprised to see me working late, so she barged in to tell me to go home and discovered Rick Carson copying my files. He gave her some excuse—that I'd asked him to fill in, he was just helping out, but Ainsley knows me too well and called to confirm his story. I showed up twenty minutes later with security and fired him on the spot."

"Sounds like a pretty strong suspect for revenge. He has a beef with you and Ainsley."

"Yeah. A week later, he sent Ainsley a strobing gif in an email—Ainsley is epileptic and extremely photosensitive, and everyone in the office knew it. The lights on our drones don't flash—they flow from one color to another—out of respect for her and others with photo sensitivities. She suffered a seizure in the office after opening the email. He was arrested and charged with assault. He pled guilty last summer to a misdemeanor."

"Where is Rick Carson now?"

"I don't know. But I'll email Detective Brown and ask him to find out." She shook her head. "If Rick tried to run me down yesterday and went after Ainsley, he must know he'd be the first suspect."

"Which is why we can't stop there. How big is HH?"

"We're pretty small, at least on the technical end. A few dozen employees in the main office. There's warehouse and distribution too, but China does all our manufacturing."

"You know everyone?"

"In the main office, yes."

"And you liked working there until yesterday?"

"Yes. It's a diverse company with several women executives. Plus the co-owner, Michelle Hollis, is Black. So the atmosphere was good for women—which can be really hard to find in tech. My issues with Dex weren't actually a big deal, because in the end, I was the boss and he knew he had to listen to me.

"What are your thoughts on Tim Hathaway?"

"He's not as smart as Michelle, but he was smart enough to team with her. He can be something of a blowhard, but he surrounds himself with good people and listens when it matters. He's always wanted Dex to run the AI development team—and he made it clear he thought the fiasco with Rick was my fault. Michelle insisted I stay on as head of AI, and that was that. But now, with my firing, he—and Dex—got their wish, and there isn't anything Michelle can do about it, because the military made the call."

"What did Tim and Michelle think of you taking the military contract? I would think losing a key player as sales were skyrocketing would be a problem."

"I think Tim wanted to send Dex to Washington, but the Navy wanted me. My work on Peacemaker was supposed to be done once the product shipped, so there was no reason to keep me in Philly when I could earn far more for HH if my military prototype could do half of what we promised."

"Was Dex mad you got the job?"

"Probably, but it was the military's choice. They wanted the Peacemaker coder, and that was me."

"Who else works under you?"

"Dex Lowery, Kevin Marks, Jessica Griggs, Raju Singh, and Piper Lee."

"Any of them have a beef with you or the company? Aside from Dex and Rick?"

"I don't know. Kevin has a giant ego—like so many white twenty-seven-year-old males in tech—but in general, he can back it up. He really *is* that smart. But he makes mistakes and can be pretty whiney instead of acknowledging it and moving on. I've worked with dozens of guys like him over the years, and they usually improve with age and experience, but not always. I hope I'm not wrong about Kevin, because I was the one who hired him."

"Any of the others a problem?"

"Not really. Raju has only been with HH about eighteen months. He works hard, meets his deadlines. Jessica has been there for three years. She and Dex bicker. He'll lose it if she advances ahead of him, but she's easier to work with even if she doesn't quite have his skills. Piper is good. She's young—only twenty-two—but she knows her stuff. She was hired to replace Rick and started about ten months ago. Peacemaker was in the bag, so she never worked on it. She's working on next year's big thing with Raju and Kevin."

"Dex and Jessica are still on Peacemaker?"

"It's mostly Dex with Jessica working on her own project and pitching in as needed. Dex's job has been to make sure the updates to Peacemaker will go smoothly as two million people launch their new drones on the same day."

"Except you said you did that."

"Yes. Dex broke it, and technically, he should have pulled Kevin in for the fix—he's the only other person in the office with skills at that level, but I fixed it." She grinned at him. "In a way, you could say I saved Christmas." She let out a sigh. "I hate the idea of missing the show at Nationals Park. Hathaway-Hollis is holding a private reception in some of the presidential suites at the stadium. Given that I was fired, I have a feeling I've been uninvited."

"But the venue holds what—thirty, forty thousand people?"

"Yes. And this isn't a ticketed event. Anyone can walk in off the street and attend. Food vendors will be open, and there will be games and other events for the kids starting at noon."

"So basically, you could go and no one could turn you away."

She smiled at that. Yes, she could show up with the crowd and avoid the employers who'd betrayed her right before the massive event she'd made possible. "Yes."

"Then we'll go."

"Really? That simple?"

"It's what you want for Christmas—er, Hanukkah, right?"

"Yes."

"Then we'll go," he repeated. "I want to see what your amazing brain has created."

She snuggled into his extra-long arms. "Thank you, Hawk."

"You like calling me that," he whispered against her temple.

"It's hot," she whispered back. "It seems like there should be birds of prey in the 'Twelve Days of Christmas' song."

"I think all the birds in the song are food. That's why they're presents."

"*I* like to eat Hawk."

He let out a sharp laugh. She joined him, feeling lighter, warmer. She hadn't realized how much she wanted to go to Nationals Park until it was decided they could.

Their laugher settled, but they remained entwined on the couch, watching the candles burn down. She felt warm, cared for, and knew Nate "Hawk" Sifuentes was the best holiday gift she'd ever received.

Chapter Ten

*D*ecember twenty-fourth began in the best way possible as Nate woke to the feel of Leah's hands on his body. He made love to her in a way that started slow, sleepy, and languid, but ended hot, fast, and intense. Afterward, he held her by his side, his heart slowly settling into an easy, post-orgasmic rhythm.

She traced the edges of the hawk wing on his stomach. "Are we going to DC today?"

He nodded. He hated giving up their sanctuary, but they could get more answers in the city than hiding out here, and it would be easier to get to Nationals Park tomorrow if they were already in the area. But finding a decent hotel room in DC on Christmas Eve might be impossible. "I'm going to talk to my boss and see if I can bring you to the compound. If that fails, we can crash at my brother's house."

"He's going to freak, isn't he? HH is his client—and a lucrative one. I'm pretty much the enemy."

"Freddy'll get over it." He ran his hand over Leah's bare bottom. Freddy had called and asked Nate to do a two-hour job just two days and one lifetime ago. Now Nate didn't want to imagine a world in which he woke up without Leah in his bed.

But that didn't mean Leah was on the same page, and he wasn't about to push it. She had bigger concerns. Starting with the woman who died in the HH townhouse. "If the dead woman is Ainsley, they'll have identified her by now. We should check the headlines."

Leah pulled on panties and a T-shirt while he donned the sweatpants again. Together, they entered the chilly living room. She grabbed the new laptop while he made coffee.

"What's the word?" he asked after a few minutes.

"Nothing at all about the fire."

"Any statement from HH?"

"Nope. But I would imagine they're trying to stay out of the news right now. The only headlines they want are drone sales."

"Yeah, I wondered why they'd fire you right before the big event, given the potential for negative publicity."

"But technically, HH hasn't fired me. The military did, and HH has me on unpaid leave while they review what I did wrong at the Navy Yard."

"Could this be all about money? Taking away your stock options before the IPO and using the military to do it?"

"It's possible, but I've ridden the startup pony before, that's why I asked for a big salary up front and fewer options."

"What about a holiday bonus?"

"I locked that down in my contract. I made all my deadlines, and we sold the baseline number of units by Cyber Monday. They have to pay me, fired or not."

"But they'll try to get out of it."

"Of course they will." She smiled. "But I'm rich. I can afford a good attorney."

He laughed, dropped a kiss on her lips, and handed her a steaming cup of coffee before turning to the cold hearth. "You should check the phone. See if Detective Brown has called with an update."

*L*eah reached for the phone, feeling trepidation. She wanted to know, and she didn't. Right now, she could still hope Ainsley was alive.

She checked voicemail, seeing a message had been left thirty minutes ago.

She called the number, and Detective Brown

answered immediately. "This is Leah Ellis. I have you on speakerphone to include Nathaniel Sifuentes."

"Ms. Ellis, I wanted to share our findings with you before the press release goes out," Brown said in his deep baritone voice. "We're still waiting on toxicology and other tests, but we have a preliminary determination based on the opinions of the arson investigator and medical examiner. Both have come to the conclusion that the fire that caused the death of Ainsley Weisz was an accident."

The kick in the gut she felt at the confirmation the woman was Ainsley was compounded by shock at the determination. "What? An accident? But how?"

"It appears Ms. Weisz was cooking with hot oil. From the ingredients, the ME believes she was making latkes when she suffered a seizure. You mentioned in your email last night that Ms. Weisz is epileptic."

Her brain swirled with questions, but she managed to say, "Yes, but her seizures are controlled with medication. The one at work had been deliberately caused by a strobe."

"The toxicology tests will take a few more days, but it's possible she missed a dose or the effectiveness of the medication was negated by other factors. I understand she was under a lot of stress with the organizing of the Peacemaker events."

"I assume. I hadn't seen her in weeks."

"We can't be certain she suffered a seizure, but it fits with the findings—her tongue was severely bitten. The cause of death, however, was smoke inhalation."

"How could her seizure trigger the fire?"

"When Ms. Weisz collapsed, she may have knocked the handle of the pan filled with boiling oil. Oil spilled all over the cooktop, including on a dish towel near the burner and another hanging on the oven door. The arson investigator believes the burner remained on and the remaining oil in the pan exceeded the flash point. Vapor ignited. The oil-soaked towels helped spread the flames. It likely took some time for the fire to take off to the degree you and Mr. Sifuentes smelled the smoke, but once that happened, the kitchen was engulfed."

Leah ran a hand over her face. Her heart ached, thinking of Ainsley, seizing and helpless as the flames spread. "Was she still alive when we first smelled the smoke?"

"Probably not. As I said, it took time for the fire to spread, but the kitchen would have filled with smoke quickly, and she was right next to the source."

He might be lying. A kindness to ease guilt and pain. She wiped at a tear. She'd had twenty-four hours to prepare for news of Ainsley's death, but such news would always hit hard. Could it really be just a freak accident, though? The timing didn't make sense.

"Wait. The townhouse was dark when we saw it before the fire started. The kitchen lights should have been on if she was cooking."

"But the kitchen is in the back of the middle floor. You might not have seen lights from the front."

It was possible. The middle floor of the townhouse was something of a tunnel. There were no windows on the sides of the building, just front and back, and a swinging door separated the kitchen from the small dining room nestled between the kitchen and living room. With the door closed, little light would slip through—and smoke would stay trapped in the kitchen.

"But...how could Ainsley be in the townhouse making latkes when the NSA had seized it?"

"That's one of the reasons I wanted to talk to you. We went several rounds with NSA and your supervisors at the Navy Yard before we found someone who would go on record. It appears the NSA never received any orders from the military to search the townhouse. It was never scheduled to be seized or locked down as far as we can confirm. And your supervisor at the Navy Yard says he was informed you were to be terminated, but he didn't order it and he doesn't know who did."

"So...who fired me?"

"Given that we're dealing with national security issues, I can't say for certain, because it's possible people in the know just won't talk to me, but as far as I can tell, your contract with the US military was never terminated. At least, not by them."

Chapter Eleven

*L*eah felt numb. She'd assumed someone in Hathaway-Hollis had pressured the military, but it was possible the military hadn't fired her at *all*? The townhouse hadn't been seized? The car and phone had essentially been stolen from her?

She'd been lied to. Betrayed. By the company she helped build. How many long nights and weekends had she worked on the Peacemaker project?

And why had they done it? For money? So they wouldn't have to honor her stock options when the IPO rolled out someday?

Considering she was the technical brains, how well did they expect that IPO to do when word got out they'd fired her without cause?

And she could sue them for this. All she needed was someone in the military to go on record to confirm they hadn't fired her. She closed her eyes and could picture the two MPs. Could she question them? Ask them who delivered the order to escort her from the premises?

And who had they turned over those car keys to? She jolted upright and scanned the room for the FedEx box, spotting it on the bench by the door, where she'd set it Sunday night. She'd placed the Mt. Vernon ticket in the box after fleeing the townhouse fire.

"Why is that important?" Nate asked.

"When I saw the MPs, I panicked. The beta test was incomplete, and someone who knew what they were doing could corrupt it. So I buried the code in the system, then deleted my files from the main directory."

"Buried your code. You mean it's not gone?"

"No. Not with this."

"I don't understand. That's for Mt. Vernon."

She pointed to the extra QR code. "This is the file path for where the code is buried."

He gave her what she'd come to think of as a hawkish grin. "Nice."

"Thank you. Frankly, I just couldn't bear to garbage my work. And I needed backup in case I was way off base on why the two MPs were there."

"But you weren't."

"No. Except…*they* were. I was never fired. But they collected my keys and cell phone, which means someone needed to claim them. It would draw attention if my personal belongings remained unclaimed because I'd never really been fired. Also worth noting, one of the things I had to leave behind was the schematic for the system I'd been building. Whoever takes over the project for the Navy would want that notebook. That would probably be Dex, given that the HH contract isn't canceled."

"Why don't you ask him?"

"I will, but first I'd like to go to the Navy Yard and speak to the MPs. They'll have a log of who they gave my phone and keys to. I'm going to need evidence to show Michelle Hollis to prove Dex and Tim sabotaged me and, by extension, HH."

"Sounds like a good starting point."

They were on the road heading back to the DC area within thirty minutes. Nate drove while Leah made calls. She put the phone on speaker so he could hear both sides of the conversations.

First, she called Michelle Hollis. "Michelle, it's Leah. It appears the military never fired me, so I just wanted to give you the heads-up that I've contacted an attorney. My car, phone, and residence were seized without cause. I was terminated without cause. HH is going to pay."

"You would do this to us right now, after what happened to Ainsley?" Hollis said.

"I'm broken up about Ainsley. But that doesn't change what HH did. It only raises more questions. Like how is it that she was in the townhouse after I'd been told no one could enter it until after the NSA searched it? Tim said it would be days before I could claim my things."

"I don't know anything about what Tim said."

"How embarrassing, considering your name is also on the company. He was speaking *for you*."

"I didn't find out that you'd been fired until after it happened. I took three damn hours off for the first time in months so I could go Christmas shopping for my kids."

"That doesn't change the fact that the military didn't fire me, Tim Hathaway did. Or why Ainsley was in a supposedly locked-down apartment."

"She probably didn't know you'd been fired either. She was in DC, dealing with vendors for the Nationals Park event. She told me it was your first Hanukkah without your mother, and she wanted to surprise you."

Leah sucked in a sharp breath and pressed her hand to her heart. Nate put a hand on her leg but kept his eyes on the road.

"Why was I fired, Michelle? And don't give me some bullshit line about missing a deadline."

"Why do you think I'd say anything when you've already told me you plan to sue?"

The muscle under Nate's hand stiffened, but Leah's voice was calm. "You don't even know, do you?"

There was a long silence, then Hollis said, "I was told the Navy was unhappy the beta test was behind schedule."

"I was behind because I had to fix Peacemaker."

"Peacemaker wouldn't have needed fixing if you hadn't screwed it up."

Leah's hand dropped on top of Nate's, sandwiching him between her thigh and palm. He turned his hand over and intertwined their fingers.

"This is all bullshit, Michelle, and you know it. The Navy never fired me. And I didn't screw up Peacemaker."

"There was nothing I could do. You were fired before I knew about it."

"Yet you didn't try to contact me after it was a done deal."

"I didn't know how to reach you. And you didn't call me either."

"I shouldn't have had to reach out to *you*. I was the one who'd been screwed. At least Dex had the brains to use my web email to try to find me."

Nate knew Leah was fishing with that line.

"Dex emailed you?"

"What did it take to get you to agree? Or was this all Tim?"

"I would never betray you like that," Hollis said.

"I know Peacemaker would have been garbage without you."

Nate returned his hand to the steering wheel and smiled. He'd known Leah was good, but was still impressed with how she'd gotten the company cofounder to join her side.

"Dex was always angry he wasn't named top engineer," Leah said.

"Dex is blinded by belief in his own greatness."

"Yet, he's the head of *my* department now, isn't he? Crazy that it happened as Peacemaker launches. He'll get all the credit."

"That's not what this is about, Leah."

"Isn't it, though? Tomorrow, when two million drones fly in perfect synchronicity, you're really going to say to the world, 'This is all thanks to the work of Leah Ellis, who was fired by HH on Sunday, and oh, by the way, we're going to roll out that IPO soon, too bad we got rid of our lead engineer'?"

The line went silent.

Leah pushed. "We both know when Dex steps forward to take a bow, you'll clap along with the rest of them."

"I've given my life to this company."

"So have I. The only difference between you and me, is you can't be fired. Think about that, and how much you can trust Tim and Dex. They'd stab you in the back too, if they could."

Again, Michelle Hollis said nothing.

"I have one last question for you," Leah said. "What time was it when HH was supposedly informed I was being fired?"

"Why does that matter?"

"Humor me."

A heavy sigh sounded from the phone. "The message I got from Tim was left around noon. Tim said he'd just received a call from Captain Sullivan with the news that you were being terminated for failing to meet Friday's beta test deadline."

Nate shifted his gaze from the road for a brief glance at Leah. "I got the call from my brother at eight a.m. He gave me your last name, the time, and the place. He specifically said HH—and not the military—was the client."

Leah directed her voice at the cell phone. "Nate was hired to pick me up after being canned. He knew at eight Sunday morning. Supposedly before Tim knew. Before you knew. And from what the police told me, before Captain Sullivan knew."

Chapter Twelve

Thirty minutes from the city, Leah's cell phone rang. She looked at the screen. "Detective Brown's number."

"Better answer it," Nate said.

"Detective Brown, I have you on speaker," she said.

"Good. We have a new development in the investigation into Ms. Weisz's death. Can you meet us at your townhouse?"

"Certainly. I can be there in a half hour. What's going on?"

"I'd rather wait until you're here to explain."

Nate hit the accelerator. Instinct told him whatever Brown had to tell them was bad. But then, good news could be delivered over the phone, so it wasn't exactly a brilliant deduction.

When they reached the townhouse complex, he

drove toward the back, finding the road blocked off by a police car and crime scene tape before he could get to Leah's street. He didn't think this was a result of the fire the other night.

He pulled to the side and parked right in front of a "No Parking" sign. He and Leah climbed out and approached the white male officer standing in front of his vehicle behind the yellow tape.

"Leah Ellis," she said to the officer. "Detective Brown called me."

"Yes, ma'am." He looked at Nate. "And you are?"

"Nate Sifuentes."

The officer spoke into the radio clipped to his collar, then said, "Detective Brown is on his way."

A moment later, a Black man in plain clothes but visibly wearing a holster and badge rounded the bend in the street. At seeing Leah and Nate, he waved them through, and the white officer nodded, allowing them to pass.

"I don't like this," Leah said, anxiety in her voice. "I think if they'd decided to treat Ainsley's death as a homicide, this isn't how they'd go about it."

Nate agreed and didn't like it either. "Something else happened."

They shook hands with the detective, then he turned and headed toward Ainsley's street, which was around another corner. "With the irregularities and questions behind your firing, I came back to the townhouse this morning to have a look around. I'm not comfortable with the accidental fire determination but need evidence to support opening a murder investigation given the initial finding." He waved toward the townhouse as they rounded the corner and it came into view. "My first surprise when I got here this morning was seeing a car parked in your driveway."

Leah let out a gasp, which could have been triggered by the ring of police cars, the sight of the burnt structure, or the crime scene unit, but she didn't leave Nate wondering. "That's my company car."

"I thought so and wanted you to confirm. The plate is wrong—probably stolen. I was going to run the VIN, but got sidetracked by my next discovery."

"You found something inside," Nate said, nodding to the scorched and water-stained townhouse. Given the array of police cars, he'd have expected to see more people outside, perhaps combing through the sedan that shouldn't be in the driveway. But they weren't here, which meant they must be inside. A precarious decision, considering the charred structure with holes cut into the side of the building, which must have been done by firefighters in their effort to stop the blaze. The back half of the second floor couldn't be structurally sound, but at least a half dozen people were inside.

"Yes. This morning, I found *someone* inside."

A flash behind the front window caught Nate's eye, and he saw the back of a person taking photos of something deeper inside the room.

Detective Brown continued, "A nude white male, probably early thirties, dark hair, medium stature, is hanging from the center beam in the living room. The body was still warm when I discovered him an hour ago."

"Oh my God," Leah said.

"I was here last night, going over the scene with the arson investigator, and there was no car in the driveway nor a dead guy hanging in the living room. Given that and the temperature of the body, he was hanged sometime in the night." The detective's gaze fixed on Leah. "A suicide note was taped to his chest. It was addressed to you, Leah. Among other things, it says 'Ainsley was an accident. I'm sorry.' I can't share the rest of the contents of the note at this time."

"Your description of the body could fit either Dexter Lowery or Rick Carson," Leah said.

"Knowing Carson has a record for assaulting Weisz, we were able to find him pretty quick through his attorney. He lives in Baltimore now. I spoke to him this morning, and he's got an alibi for Sunday, but I still plan to interview him in person later today." Detective Brown nodded toward the upper window. "As far as the body inside, there was no ID on him, and his face is—let's just say hanging isn't a pretty way to die. Blood and DNA will tell us definitively. For right now, we're just looking for a preliminary ID to get the ball rolling." The detective glanced from Leah to Nate and said, "From the contents of the note…I have reason to believe you can describe Dexter Lowery's tattoo?"

Leah gripped Nate's hand and squeezed. "Dex has a blue frog on his"—she closed her eyes and paused before adding—"left buttock."

Nate felt a twinge in his chest area. The hand in his squeezed tighter. He squeezed back, telling his shitty ego it was none of his damn business.

"Thank you. I need to speak with one of the investigators. I'll be right back. I have more questions." The detective jogged the short distance to the front door, then hurried up the steps to the main floor, where Dexter Lowery hung like a chandelier in the remains of Leah's burned-out townhouse.

She turned to face him. "I can explain."

"You don't owe me an explanation at all." And she didn't. Although it might have been nice if she'd told him the exact nature of her relationship with the man she'd named as her prime suspect in this ordeal.

"I do. And not because I slept with him, but because I didn't tell you about it." She sighed. "Last December, after the company holiday party. I'd just wrapped the Peacemaker project and we were making plans to launch it this season if the betas went well. The military was in talks with HH to hire me. I'd just fired Rick, and my mom had just died. I drank too much and broke my number one rule and slept with Dex." She ran a hand over her face. "It was so stupid. I didn't even like the guy, but he was being all nice and I was lonely. I woke up the next day with a splitting headache and horrified. I reported it to Michelle —the company doesn't have fraternization rules, so I knew I wouldn't get in trouble, but he's my subordinate, and rules or no rules, I shouldn't have done it. I also wanted it on record with HR so we'd have a process if disputes arose. I did every-thing by the book, and it pissed Dex off that he couldn't use it against me. He'd hoped I'd try to hold it as a dirty secret he could blackmail me with."

"He took advantage of you when you were grieving and drunk so he could have leverage over you?"

"Grieving and drunk were factors—which is why I mentioned them—but it's still something *I* did. I wasn't too impaired for consent. He doesn't get a pass—he shouldn't have done it either—and once I realized his motives, I was even more appalled, but it only made my own guilt worse. I was so stupid."

"I think you need to cut yourself some slack." He meant it even though it bothered him she'd held back this not so fun fact.

"I'm sorry I didn't tell you. It's…part of being ashamed it happened."

"It could be another motive he had to be after your job."

"Yes." She turned to face the townhouse. "Did Dex kill himself because he'd accidently—or purposely—killed Ainsley? Or were they both murdered?"

Chapter Thirteen

etective Brown managed to get confirmation from the Navy Yard MPs that Dexter Lowery had arrived at the Navy Yard to claim Hathaway-Hollis property including Leah's company cell phone and vehicle. The MP who signed over the property remembered the man had argued for claiming the sketchbook and copy of Leah's Mt. Vernon ticket, but the MPs had refused on the grounds that neither were HH property.

After answering the rest of Detective Brown's questions, they were free to go. Leah was not under suspicion in Dex's death, as the man had strangled to death within the last several hours and cell phone records could prove she and Nate were in a cabin two hours away during the window of opportunity.

They returned to the car and settled inside, but Nate didn't start the engine. He just stared at the police car blocking the road.

"What are you thinking about?"

"If Dex was at the Navy Yard trying to get your notebook, he couldn't be the guy in the gray sedan."

She stiffened. "I hadn't thought of that. Dex has an alibi of sorts." She bit her lip, remembering that night. She'd thought the gray sedan was made-up bullshit invented by Nate to get her to go along with him. She'd assumed he was after military secrets or something. What a long road they'd traveled in a few short days.

"I never actually saw the sedan," she admitted. "Not even when it tried to run me down. I saw a blur and trees and bricks when you tackled me, and heard the screech of tires."

"I didn't really see it then either. I heard the engine gun and…it's something I train soldiers for. The sounds that happen right before things go to hell. We run simulations to hone instincts and reduce reaction time."

"It saved my life."

"Maybe. Or maybe the driver just wanted to scare you."

"I don't buy the accidental-fire-and-death finding. Could the gray sedan have gotten from Mt. Vernon to the townhouse with enough time for the driver to kill Ainsley and start the fire before we got there?"

"Easily. We spent a lot of time talking before we hit the road, then we parked several blocks away from the townhouse and walked. The gray sedan had forty-five minutes on us, give or take."

"But it's also true that Dex could have left the Navy Yard with my car and driven straight to the townhouse and killed Ainsley."

"Yes. He doesn't have an alibi for that, and his suicide note takes the blame."

"Yeah, always convenient when a supposed suicide confesses to an unsolved murder that's been deemed an accident."

"Detective Brown didn't seem to be buying it either—but investigators have to consider every possibility. I gathered that the fact you could describe the frog tattoo confirmed a reference to your relationship in the suicide note."

"It wasn't a relationship," she said under her breath. Damn Dex for making it an issue even in death. There were few things she regretted as much as that awful night. She leaned her head against the cool glass of the window. "At least they're going to thoroughly investigate Ainsley's death now."

Nate's hand found hers. "We're cool, Leah. Past is past. I've slept with people I wish I hadn't too. You don't need anyone's forgiveness except your own."

She squeezed his hand. If only it were that easy. About the only thing worse than sleeping with a prick like Dex would be taking advantage of one of her more vulnerable subordinates, like Kevin.

"There's something really messed up going on with your company," Nate said.

"I can't believe they're going to go on with the event at Nationals Park tomorrow, but at the same time, there's no way they can stop it."

"It seems like someone is trying to sabotage the company. Your firing. Ainsley's death. Now Dex's supposed suicide. I mean, it could be a simple power play by Dex gone wrong. Maybe he did commit suicide—but he still had reason to believe Ainsley's death would be written off as an accident, so the timing doesn't make sense in that scenario."

"None of it makes sense. No one on the inside has motive to sabotage the company—least of all Dex, who was making a play for my job with Tim's full support."

"The disgruntled former employee angle seems a little too pat, but it's not lost on me that Carson is nearby in Baltimore. Did he have a beef with Dex too?"

"Not that I know of."

Nate put the car in gear and made a U-turn and headed for the main road.

"Where are we going?" she asked. They didn't need to go to the Navy Yard now that they knew what happened to her car and other confiscated items.

"The compound, unless you've got a better idea?"

"Nope. We can leave interrogating Carson to the professionals."

"You think it's him?"

"Honestly, no clue. He always claimed he didn't send the gif to Ainsley, but forensic examination of his computer proved otherwise."

After a mile of driving, Nate said, "Detective Brown said Dex was nude with the note taped to his chest. The thing about a hanging death while naked is it's usually determined to be autoerotic asphyxiation resulting in accidental death. There's an extra humiliation factor to being found that way. But this guy died in a house that was *already* a crime scene, and he was wearing his suicide note. So it can't be an accident. Yet the humiliation is there."

Leah gasped and sat up straight. "You're right. Dex Lowery never would have killed himself that way."

"Whoever killed him hated him. Intensely. Wanted him to take the blame for Ainsley's death and be humiliated at the same time." He pulled into a parking lot at a strip mall, parked, and faced her. "And this is personal, directed at you too. You lost your job. Your home. Your car. Your friend. And I don't think the killer hated Ainsley. She wasn't humiliated. She might've been incidental—even accidental, which argues against Carson. But still, two murders happened in the townhouse you were living in. Dex didn't have to die there, but it sure as hell sends a message that he did."

Nate was right. It was all directed at her, including an email that called her traitor, whore, bitch, and slut. Plus, the suicide note had been addressed to her.

"After taking away your job, friend, and home, what's left?"

"I don't have family. So all that's left is—" Her body went cold at the obvious answer. "My reputation."

"Yes."

Her heart pounded at the implication. "The drones. The show. The Christmas Day Peacemaker protocol."

Chapter Fourteen

"Could the protocol be altered?" Nate asked. "Dex could do it. His job was to ensure the firmware could handle the flood of updates that will happen tomorrow and make sure the code for the December 25 Drone Dance works. He pushed a lot of that on me, and I did it because I didn't want him to screw it up. But he had access to everything."

"We can't rule out that Dex was working on his own. He got you fired. He altered the code and killed himself once his work was done." Nate didn't believe it, but he knew ruling things out too soon was the best way to miss something important.

"It's also possible that once the Peacemaker code was altered, Dex was no longer needed," Leah said.

"Agreed." To him, that was the most likely

scenario: Dex had outlived his usefulness, but not for very long. A few hours at most.

"Dex, or whoever, could have taken my computer and Peacemaker notebook from the townhouse on Sunday and surprised Ainsley—I'd finished my last update at two a.m., and my notebook was right next to the laptop. With the schematic, it would be easier to break down what I'd done and change it."

"Does Rick Carson have the skills to change the protocol?" he asked.

"Yes. He worked on Peacemaker from the start."

Nate pulled back onto the roadway. "Can you check the protocol, see if it's been altered?"

"If I had drones. I need at least three."

Nate called Keith as he drove and gave him a brief rundown of the situation and requested permission to bring Leah into the compound and give her access to the computer network. Keith agreed and said he was fairly certain his wife got him a drone for Christmas, which he'd bring to the compound.

Next, Nate called his brother and asked if the twins were getting HH drones for Christmas. Freddy hemmed and hawed and finally admitted he'd purchased two at the beginning of the holiday frenzy and had debated selling them on eBay as demand grew, but then the twins had seen the commercials and wanted to go to Nationals Park—

with or without drones, but of course, the kids made it clear all their Christmas dreams would come true if their own drones were part of the Christmas Day extravaganza.

Over the speakerphone, Freddy added, "By the way, damn you, Leah. I wanted to spend Christmas Day at home, drinking spiked coffee, eating treats made by my kids in the new Easy Bake Oven, and crushing Nate in the video game I *know* he got me for Christmas, but instead I have to take the Metro to Nationals Park with my family to watch drones dance. And I know it will be amazing, but I'm still pissed. It's Christmas. No one wants to leave the house on Christmas."

Leah laughed. "Sorry. The Christmas Day events weren't my bright idea. I designed the dance, but I'm not in marketing."

"So now you want to steal my kids' biggest Christmas presents. The ones Santa was going to get credit for. While I smile and point to the Easy Bake Oven to prove Daddy loves them."

"Hey now, Santa taking credit *definitely* isn't my fault. And I need drones but I won't steal them. I'll give both your kids an entire platoon of drones and every Easy Bake Oven ever made, new-in-box, if you help me."

"So basically, you want to outdo me and Santa combined. Now, I'm generally opposed to this idea, but I do love spoiling my kids, so I'm willing to negotiate."

"I will set up college funds for both of them. Four years. In state, out of state. Private, public. Doesn't matter. My accountant will handle it."

"The drones are yours."

Nate laughed. "That's a little more than the going rate on eBay."

She shrugged. "I can't think of a better way to spend my money."

To Freddy, Nate said, "Bring the drones to the compound. We're almost there."

"See you soon, bro."

Nate hit the End button on the phone and gripped Leah's hand, a warm feeling hitting him at the idea she was about to meet his brother.

"You and Freddy are close," she said.

"Yeah. We're only two years apart in age. Growing up, he was my big brother and best friend."

"I'm jealous. I always wanted a sister or brother."

He lifted their entwined fingers and kissed the back of her hand. "You can borrow Freddy. His wife, Angelica, is pretty great too."

She turned in the passenger seat and faced him. "Are you…offering to share your family with me?"

"Will you do me the honor of taking my brother off my hands?"

She laughed. "I like you, Nathaniel Sifuentes."

"What happened to 'Hawk'?"

"I'm saving that for when you soar."

"Oh, so that's how this is going to be."

"You're only as good as my last orgasm."

"I will rise to the occasion."

"I know you will."

He laughed.

Before they reached the compound, he called Josh and Chase and asked them to track down any operatives who had purchased HH drones for the holidays. Everyone who lived in the compound was single, and with low living expenses, they could afford to indulge themselves during the holidays. He'd bet more than one bought themselves a drone for Christmas.

They arrived, and, after dumping their shopping bags of clothes and other odds and ends in his quarters, she grabbed her fancy new computer and he led her to the gymnasium, where they had both a basketball and indoor tennis court.

"Tennis?" she asked. "I didn't think that was a big military sport."

"Robert Beck had a passion for tennis. There was an indoor court in the Alaska compound too."

"Do you play?"

"I enjoy it, but I'm terrible at it," he said.

"It's good to do things you like even if you aren't an expert. I think most adults forget that and give up some of life's pleasures."

He wrapped an arm around her waist and pulled her to him. "And what do you enjoy but you aren't very good at? Because as far as I can tell, you're pretty damn great at everything."

He dropped a light kiss on her lips.

"I'm terrible at watching TV. But I do it anyway."

He laughed. "How can you be terrible at watching TV? It's not even a skill."

"Oh, it's a skill. I talk over all the dialogue—even when I'm alone—yelling at the characters when they're wrong. And then I have to rewind and figure out what I missed when yelling. And sometimes, if I can't take it, I'll look up the show I'm watching online and read all the spoilers."

He shook his head and laughed. "Okay. Remind me not to watch TV with you."

"No way. You're stuck with me, bad TV watching and all. I'm very good at other things, which makes up for it."

"That you are," he murmured, then he kissed her. A deep kiss that made promises for later.

"Enough of that, Hawk," Chase said from the doorway. "There's no mistletoe in here." He shook his head. "You've defiled my cabin, haven't you?"

Leah burst out laughing as they separated.

Nate said, "Sorry, man. Yeah. Maybe. A little bit."

Chase clapped him on the back. "You owe me. So much."

Leah kissed his cheek. "Thank you for everything."

"I hear you need some drones," Josh said, entering the room with Tricia Rooks. They each carried a box with the bright red HH logo. "We found two."

Leah's face lit up, probably brighter than any kid's would on Christmas Day. Never in his life had a woman's smile made his heart squeeze in quite that way.

*L*eah lined up the five drones in the center of the basketball court. A dozen people stood at the edge of the room, among them Josh, Chase, Freddy, and Keith. The rest were Raptor operatives who lived in the compound.

"For the first test, we'll work with the preloaded firmware," she said to her audience.

Each drone came with a motion-sensitive wand controller, the size and shape of a high-end smartphone with a two-inch screen to view images recorded by the drone's camera.

Leah looped the strap for two controllers on each wrist and offered Nate the fifth controller. She showed him the basic motions to control movement by setting one of her drones in flight. It followed her movements perfectly, stopping only when her motion would send it crashing into the ground or other object. Like a self-driving car, it could redirect.

He copied it, and his drone flew smoothly, shiny metallic silver catching the gym lights, looking like a sixties-era vision of the future as it floated in the air. The aluminum alloy housing gave the drone more heft, which required a more powerful motor that purred like a contented kitten. The end result was a bigger, beefier drone that somehow danced with the lightness of a ballerina. She'd argued for lighter, cheaper plastic with the design team, but had to admit the metal sheath and retro-futuristic look set Peacemaker apart, made it exceptional, and was as recognizable as the bright red HH logo on the side. She wasn't alone in making Peacemaker a success and needed to give the design team their due.

"Okay, that's cool," Nate said, wiggling the controller and watching the drone mimic the movement three feet away.

"Ready to test all five?" she asked.

"Ready."

"We'll launch the drones and then hit the AI button on the controller. Then they'll do a basic friendship dance to show they're communicating."

One by one, she launched her drones and turned on the AI, then she nodded to Nate to launch his. Her drones reacted to the new one, making room as starlings would for a hawk, splitting and scattering, but still they moved in synchronicity, mirroring each other.

"Hit the AI button so your hawk can make peace."

He laughed and tapped the button. The dance changed, no longer starlings and hawk, but rather five hawks, spinning and soaring.

"Wow," one of the observers said.

She couldn't help but beam. Having an audience for her art was rare.

"Bring it in," she said as she landed her four drones.

To the group, she said, "That's the basic preloaded software. Without any updates, all the drones can do that. But that's not the dance that will happen at three tomorrow. That one is a special one-time-only deal." She turned to her computer and opened a terminal that connected to the drones via Wi-Fi or cellular signal, depending on what was available, and entered a code.

"I'm now going to make these run through the basic preloaded December 25 Drone Dance sequence—D25DD. Except for powering on, the remote controls are locked out of this sequence. That way, no one can act as a spoiler and ruin the show. If the drones are powered on and flying at three p.m., they will be in AI mode."

She hit the Start button on the keyboard, and all five drones took flight and did a simple dance. This was the preloaded default, and it would be good enough for most viewers.

But most viewers didn't know what the drones could really do.

Leah cut off the sequence, and the drones landed, then she returned to the center of the gym and one by one used a pencil tip to press the Reset button on the first three devices.

"I'm triggering the drone's internal Wi-Fi or 3G connection to upload all the latest updates, including the D25DD choreography. The drones communicate with each other and share choreography, which is why I didn't reset the last two. They should follow along, receiving their performance cues from the other drones. The dance they're about to perform should be the final coding I uploaded at two a.m. Sunday."

She entered the password to run D25DD into the terminal open on her laptop. The drones took flight and the dance started well. All performances would be different depending on the number of drones involved, but these were definitely the moves she'd programmed. The sequence was a full twenty minutes long. Like any halfway-decent fireworks display, it had to last and have a few surprises.

At seven minutes in, the first drone went rogue. It left the party and shot like a rocket across the gym, aiming straight for the audience.

Leah hit the kill button, and it did a hard reverse then dropped like a stone.

She didn't take her eyes off the drones in flight,

couldn't see the faces of the onlookers, but heard their gasps as two drones first circled each other, then turned and faced the gathered audience. The lights strobed—which they absolutely should not do—and then they flew to the far end of the room—the limit of their reach—before zooming forward, charging the audience as they gathered speed. Leah used her open terminal to halt their flight before they could crash into the spectators.

At the same time, the final two drones flew erratically, tapping on the walls as if searching for a window or a door. When none could be found, they also flew to the far end of the room, then turned and charged. These drones targeted Nate and Leah—as if beckoned by the control wands. Leah hit the Kill button, and both drones halted, then dropped a few feet away.

Her heart raced as she looked at the silver drones that littered the gym floor.

They'd been programmed to attack the audience. To flash strobing lights. And to escape, or, if that wasn't possible, to attack anyone holding a wand. Who knows what they'd do if they flew beyond the reach of their controllers.

Given their greater weight and strong motors, they could seriously hurt people if the attack was targeted. Especially if they ganged up—worked in unison to attack a single spectator.

She'd been able to stop the drones because she'd

been logged in to the firmware. That wouldn't be possible for the thousands of people attending Peacemaker events across the country. Because of the AI lock, there would be no way to stop drones going berserk during the D25DD flight.

Chapter Fifteen

They gathered in a large conference room on the main floor of the compound: Keith, Nate, Josh, Chase, Leah, and Michelle Hollis, who'd driven from a hotel in DC, where all the HH executives were staying.

Leah tapped at the computer keys, and the big screen at the front of the room filled with the recording of the drones' wild flight, captured by cameras set up throughout the gym.

"How do I know you didn't program them to do that?" Hollis asked. "I know you're more than capable of it, Leah."

Leah gave her former boss a look. "Because you know me, Michelle. This is my life's work. You really think I'd do something this horrible?"

Hollis pursed her lips, then finally said, "No."

"After the initial test," Leah said, "we ran another one. Lucky for us, Raptor has a bunch of medical and other dummies they use for their trainings. We gathered every human-sized dummy we could find and set them up in the bleachers. I put all five control wands in the seats, between the dolls. This is what happened."

Leah hit play on the second video. Nate watched the scene again, as horrified seeing it on the screen as he'd been when he watched it play out in real life. The drones had targeted the child-sized dummies. They'd teamed up and dive-bombed the children like birds of prey intent on the kill.

Leah hit the Pause button, and the drones were frozen in flight, in the act of pummeling a child.

Michelle Hollis covered her mouth with her hand, her brown eyes wide with shock and horror. "They'll all do this tomorrow? All two point three million drones?"

Two point three million demon drones? *Holy hell.*

"Yes. Once one updates, it will update the others, spreading like a virus because we wanted to make it easy for customers. I hooked all five drones up to my computer and checked the code. The push update that three of them received when I hit the drone Reset button was uploaded early this morning."

Hollis dropped her face into her hands. "Who did this? Dex? Before he killed himself?"

"I think it was Dex. And maybe he killed himself. Maybe this was his grand screw-you to the company. Or it could be someone else. But I'm pretty sure whoever it was would need Dex and his computer. He had direct remote access to the files."

"So did you. Your computer could have been stolen Sunday, when Ainsley…"

"It's possible. I haven't asked what they've recovered from the townhouse. But even so, my computer, like Dex's, was locked without my face scan and thumbprint."

"So you're saying that tomorrow afternoon, two point three million drones are going to attack all the people gathered to watch them dance all across the country?"

"Yes," Leah said.

Hollis rolled her hand into a fist, and her face contorted in pain. "We have to cancel all the events."

"I can fix it," Leah said. "It will take me hours to piece together the code, but I can do it, if you give me a computer with access to the company servers. My code is still there. It's just broken apart. I can repair it. But once the repair is in place, we'll need to lock down the system to prevent whoever created the berserker code from uploading it again. They will have switched Dex's computer's biometric lock with their own once they were in."

"I need to talk to Tim about this."

Leah shook her head. "No, Michelle, there's a reason I only invited you to this meeting."

"Tim might have been behind your firing, but

there is *no way* he's behind this. This will destroy HH."

"And potentially kill thousands of people. Children," Nate said.

She met his gaze and nodded. "You're right, of course. That is far more important. But Tim Hathaway didn't write that code. He knows nothing about programming and AI."

"I agree," Leah said, "but if word gets out that I'm fixing D25DD, whoever wrote the berserker code will gut the system. Tim might talk to the wrong person. Or you might be overheard. Every engineer in the company knows how to program a surveillance drone, so it's not crazy to think someone could be listening. Hell, Raju, Piper, and Kevin have been designing spider drones for the last ten months. And you're all staying in the same hotel. Don't trust anyone. Don't trust the damn walls."

"If that's the case, they could already know I'm here."

"If anyone asks, tell them you met with me as I requested but say I'm freaking out about being fired and angry. That's what they'll hope to hear anyway."

"But only tell that lie," Nate said, "if you can be convincing. You tip whoever did this off, and Christmas is cancelled for two point three million families."

Hollis nodded, and Nate figured she was up to

the task. She was smart, and Leah said they could trust her. She proved herself when she reached into her briefcase and pulled out a laptop. "How long will this take you?"

"Probably much of the night."

"This is the only machine I brought with me to DC. You'll have to cut off remote access to the company's servers when you're done."

"I'll notify you before I do it."

"We need to change my face scan to yours." She tapped a few keys, then said, "Jesus. I can't believe I'm entrusting you with the entire company."

"It's this or delete D25DD. If that happens, not a single drone will fly tomorrow."

"We still might have to do that if you can't fix it."

"Yes."

Hollis tapped several keys, then turned the computer to Leah. "Smile for the face scan."

Once the task was completed, she rose from her seat. "I want you to know, after we spoke this morning, I called Captain Sullivan and asked about your firing. It appears he received a spoof email from his chain of command ordering your firing, so when the MPs called to confirm the order to escort you off base, he gave them the go-ahead. He was in the middle of a holiday gathering with family visiting from across the country. He didn't give it the attention he would have otherwise."

"I think that was by design. Tim and Dex never

expected the firing to be questioned," Leah said. "But then the police needed to confirm my story in the investigation into Ainsley's death."

"I don't know what I'm going to do about Tim," Hollis said. "I can't fire him. But his action destroyed our relationship with the military."

"Not to mention destroying Leah's reputation, leaving her without money, car, home, or phone in a city where she knew no one," Nate added, again pointing out that the company consequences were minimal compared to the human ones.

She met his gaze. "Again, you're right. My problem is, I don't know what consequences he'll face beyond losing the military as a client."

"If he spoofed a military email, there are legal consequences," Leah said.

"Tim doesn't have those skills. You know that was Dex."

Leah nodded.

Unsaid was the fact that Dex was dead, having paid a much higher price than the crime of spoofing a military email deserved.

"Anyway, I wanted to let you know what I learned. I will deal with Tim's power play, but I'm not sure how. Yet. Now, I need to get back to the hotel before anyone notices I took off."

"Is anyone behaving suspiciously?" Keith asked.

"Everyone is in shock over Ainsley and Dex, so it's impossible to know."

She turned to Leah. "Show up at the executive

suite right before the show and hand me the laptop. Let's see how everyone reacts." She then faced the rest of them. "You should all come. Bring your families if you want. You can be my special guests."

"Put Raptor down as extra security you've hired," Keith said. "We've got an arrangement with DC police and will be able to carry firearms into the venue if we're there in an official capacity."

Hollis nodded. "Consider it done.

*A*n hour into Leah's coding marathon, Josh and Nate stepped into the conference room. Josh held a menorah and a box of candles, and Nate held the menorah he'd purchased Sunday night for her. "I thought you might want to do it together tonight," Josh said.

Leah smiled. Without siblings, she'd always only had one menorah to light, but she knew in some families, each member had their own.

It was strange and more than a little heart-warming to feel like her family was expanding, even in this small way. After they said the blessings and lit their menorahs, Leah asked, "Do you have siblings, Josh? Family you usually do this with?"

"I have a brother, but we aren't close. He lives in Portland—Oregon—with his daughter, Ava. I feel bad I can't be there for Ava. She's having a rough time, and my brother isn't Father of the Year material. It's tough, being so far away."

"I'm sorry. Will Ava be going to a Peacemaker event tomorrow?" The Hanukkah gift market was tiny compared to the Christmas market, but Leah knew there were kids who would receive a Peacemaker tonight for Hanukkah so they could participate tomorrow. For that reason, she'd insisted there be no religious symbols in the D25DD protocol. The dance was a message of peace and friendship for all.

"I don't know. I figured I'd wait to see if you get the fix done before I ask. If you don't, I'll warn her to stay home."

"You doubting me?" she asked with a grin.

He held up his hands. "No way."

She smiled. "Well, I should get back to it if I'm going to live up to your expectations."

She settled back into the code, hardly noticing when both men left. The candles burned down, and later, Nate arrived with a plate of food she ignored. He settled in the corner and kept her company.

Finally, at two in the morning on Christmas Day, she uploaded the last of the repairs and notified Michelle before she shut down all remote access to the servers.

She'd run repeated tests with the drones. The flight was flawless. The damage fixed. It had gone quickly, all things considered, but then she'd had to do something similar—although less dire—last week.

She stood and stretched.

Nate closed the book he was reading. "That's it?" he asked.

"That's it," she confirmed. "I'll test it again in the morning, but a repair at this point would mean a trip to Philly."

"Raptor has a helicopter, if it comes to that."

"Keith said as much. We can pray we don't need it."

He pulled her onto his lap and kissed her neck.

"What would I have done if you hadn't picked me up on Sunday?"

He ran a hand through her hair. "I don't even want to think about that scenario."

She kissed him. "I just realized something."

"What's that?"

"It's Christmas." She cupped his beard in her palm. "Merry Christmas, Hawk."

"Thank you." He smiled. "I heard a rumor that you just saved Christmas."

"As a matter of fact, I *did* just save Christmas. Really and truly."

"You deserve a hero's present, so tomorrow, I want to take you back to the mountains and have a real vacation that includes walks in the woods and sex in the hot tub."

"It sounds lovely, but it might get awkward with Chase there."

He laughed and kissed her lips. "He offered it to us for the rest of the year."

"That's so kind of him. Why did he decide not to go?"

"Aside from us defiling the place?" He chuckled, then turned serious. "Chase has had a rough year, and he's always liked to escape to a quiet cabin to get away. But he told me tonight that he's not feeling the noise like he did in the past. He'd rented the cabin in case he needed it, but he's liking being among friends this holiday and knows we'll enjoy it more."

She closed her eyes and imagined escaping for a week with Nate. They could relax without questions or suspicions. No one but a few trusted people would know where they were. She'd be safe with Nate, and the detectives investigating Dex's and Ainsley's deaths could do their job. "Can we go tonight? After Christmas dinner with your family?"

"Sure. We can go before dinner if you want. Freddy will understand."

"No. I want to celebrate your holiday with your family."

"Okay, we'll head out after dinner."

They went to Nate's quarters and crawled into bed. Leah was out almost the moment her head hit the pillow. They slept for five hours, then woke up Christmas morning and made love.

She needed that connection with him, the physical and emotional release, the thrill and pleasure.

She'd have been nervous no matter what on this day. It was the crowning achievement of her professional life, but given everything else, she would be a basket case without Nate to hold on to.

Her Hawk. Her lifeline.

They shared a quiet morning in his tiny quarters. She'd forgotten to fill his stocking before bed, so she rushed to set it up while he was in the shower. All she had were a few silly puzzles and games she'd managed to grab on Monday, but she put a box of condoms in there too, which made him laugh.

They worked the puzzles and played with her dreidel and ate chocolate, but her nerves grew with each moment.

Two hours before it was time to go to the park, she tested the drones again to see if more sabotage had occurred in the night. She reset the drones again, and they flew smoothly. She released them one at a time, like birds, and watched as the dance shifted with the introduction of a new friend.

It was ready.

She showered and dressed, donning the only nice clothes she had—the outfit she'd worn Sunday. Somewhere in the Raptor compound, there was a sewing machine and a person who knew how to use it, and she was thankful for the spot cleaning and professional-looking repair Nate had managed to procure for her while she worked yesterday.

Nationals Park would open to families at noon, with the food vendors selling holiday treats, and bounce houses and other carnival-like attractions being completely free to the public. Drones weren't required to enter, but families with drones would get a special wristband and would sit in the lowest section of the park.

They'd agreed to arrive at one thirty with Freddy and his family and the two drones the kids didn't get to open that morning, so they couldn't be from Santa after all. Freddy got full credit for being a doting dad, and Nate and Leah took the blame for the delivery delay.

If Nate was nervous about the twins being at the park for the display, he didn't show it, and she appreciated his faith in her. For herself, she was nervous walking into the park, but they were normal jitters that came from the culmination of years of work in such a very public way.

The belly flutters settled when she saw the crowds of children laughing and squealing and enjoying the carnival atmosphere. She'd done this. The Peacemaker protocol hadn't been her idea, but she'd brought it to life, making this event possible.

She got a little thrill seeing all the parents holding drones as the kids bounced in bounce houses and played tag on the baseball field. There had to be five thousand people in the concourse alone.

The crowds, the excitement, that was Ainsley's work. This event was her crowning achievement as much as D25DD was Leah's. "I wish Ainsley could see this."

Nate wrapped an arm around her shoulders. "I wish I'd had a chance to meet her."

"I don't understand why someone would destroy everything we've been working on. I mean, for starters, we'll all make money if today goes off without a hitch. Every single employee has stock options, and the company already made money hand over fist this holiday season."

"Which makes Rick Carson the prime suspect."

"But he's obvious and smart enough to know it. How would he think he'd get away with sabotaging Peacemaker? With killing Ainsley?"

"Why did he think he'd get away with sending a flashing gif to Ainsley in the first place?" Nate asked.

"He claimed he was framed."

"And maybe he was. So if not Rick, who? Some people are more into revenge than money, and this feels like revenge to me. Specifically in the way it focused around you." He stopped in his tracks and tugged on her hand, then pulled her to the side, away from the crowds. "Is there anyone at work who's hit on you and you turned them down?"

"Aside from Dex? Not…really."

"Not really. What does that mean?"

"A few times, Kevin would say something, like maybe it was a joke or maybe he was flirting. But it was awkward. Around the third or so time it happened, I shut him down. I made it clear I neither date nor flirt with coworkers. I was his supervisor, there is no such thing as 'harmless' flirting in that circumstance. Plus, I'm too old for him."

"How did he handle it?"

"He said I misunderstood. He wasn't flirting. I overreacted. Threatened to go to HR and let them know I made him feel uncomfortable and was making up stories about him. I ended up going to HR and filed my own report."

"When was this?"

"Six months ago? Last summer sometime, definitely."

"So you told him you don't date coworkers. Do you think he found out about Dex and you? Could that have set him off? You rejected him, then he finds out that the reason you gave was just an excuse"—he held up a hand—"in his mind. I know it wasn't just an excuse."

"You mean, is Kevin…an incel?" She'd read articles about incel—involuntary celibate—men, some of whom used the label to justify their misogyny, even violence, toward women who didn't give them the sex they believed was their due.

"Yes, that's exactly what I mean."

"I honestly never looked at him as anything other than an egotistical coder. I've never thought about his sexuality, sexual experience, or lack thereof. He was just a person I had to remind on a weekly basis that even the best football players have to show up and take direction from their coach."

"I trained that kind of guy a thousand times in Alaska. Some were definitely incels, confused why women didn't want to spend time with them, when they were difficult assholes no one wanted to be around."

She took his hand and led him through a tunnel to the bleachers. "Let's find seats." She lifted the satchel holding Michelle's laptop. "We can take a look at his social media."

They took two seats at the end of a row, and Leah logged in and started browsing. She easily found his social media accounts, but he hadn't updated those in the last several months. She then searched for accounts using variations of the screen name he used in the office message system, and hit pay dirt.

KyloKev6022x was a very lonely and angry man.

Chapter Sixteen

The words on the screen were damning. Paragraph after paragraph of misogyny. Women who didn't give KyloKev6022x the time of day were whores, bitches, and sluts, the words repeated ad nauseum. He didn't get the respect or sex that was his due, and he vented his frustration to other incels, who goaded him on to take action against the cold sluts of the world.

"This is the kind of guy," Nate said, gesturing to the screen, "who thinks the world—but most especially *you*, who had firsthand experience with his superior brain—owes him attention. And yet…you said you didn't notice him in that way at all."

She hadn't. Even when he'd seemed to be flirting with her, she hadn't taken it seriously. She was too old for him, and not just in years, but in maturity.

"Incels are the scariest," Nate said, "because

you don't notice them until they pop. And when they pop, they shoot up nightclubs, concerts, college campuses. Places women frequent."

"Or reprogram drones to attack children," Leah said, her breathing tight. Kevin had worked for her. She'd hired him. And she'd never spotted the monster within.

She forwarded the links to Kevin's social media to Detective Brown. It was Christmas Day, the man was probably enjoying the holiday with family and friends, but she wasn't surprised when he responded immediately: *Heading to Nationals Park now.*

She checked the time. He wouldn't make it before the show. "We should head up to the executive suite."

"I was thinking the same thing," Nate said.

He texted Keith, Josh, and Chase, and the three operatives met them inside the concourse by the ramp. They ascended to the luxury suites, while outside, children and their families were settling into stadium seats, preparing to release their drones. There were workers collecting drones and lining them up in rows on the field.

"How're you holding up?" Josh asked as they climbed the ramp.

"Nervous," she admitted. "I'm scared the drones won't fly at all, scared of walking into the suite and facing a killer and not knowing it."

Nate squeezed her hand. "We've got a suspect."

"Which one?" Keith asked.

She described Kevin briefly so they'd know who to look for. There was no time to say more than that, because they'd reached the suite.

Leah gave their names to the security guard. The man checked the list, then opened the door to a room that overlooked center field.

A dozen people were in the room, the rest outside in the stadium seats, separated from the room by a large window and accessible through a door to the side. Inside and out, everyone had a cocktail in hand. It wasn't the most boisterous gathering, but then, the company had lost three key employees in the last few days. The official story was one was fired, one accidental death, one suicide, but most of the people here had to know there was more to it than that.

Kevin stood near the door and was one of the first people to meet her gaze. She could swear she saw a flash of glee in his eyes.

A slow hush descended as her former coworkers spotted her. Michelle played her part to the hilt, shouting, "Leah! So glad you could make it!" She crossed the room to give her a kiss on each cheek as if nothing had happened since Leah left Philadelphia three weeks ago.

"I wanted to return your laptop," she said, hoisting it up for all to see.

Jaws dropped. Some looked confused. Kevin's look of glee transformed to hostility.

That was the reaction she'd been looking for.

Did Kevin want revenge because Leah had never expressed the slightest interest in him? If so, how would he react to Nate?

"Michelle, I'd like you to meet my boyfriend, Nate Sifuentes."

"Boyfriend?" Michelle said, and Leah blessed her natural curiosity that made her surprise genuine and obvious, even as she shook Nate's hand as if she hadn't met him the day before.

"Nice to meet you," Nate said.

"We just met on Sunday," Leah added, watching Kevin with her peripheral vision.

"That's awfully fast to be calling him your boyfriend," he said, brazenly joining the conversation. Kevin's gaze raked Nate—older, larger, and an all-around perfect example of masculine beauty—with barely concealed disgust.

She put an arm around Nate's waist, and he draped an arm over her shoulders and kissed her full on the lips, staking an obvious claim. He then met Kevin's angry gaze. "When it's right, you know it."

"And the fact that she's rich means nothing to you?"

Leah gave him a sharp glare. "I don't see how that's any of your business."

"I don't work for you anymore. I can say what I think."

Michelle frowned at him. "But you still work for me."

Kevin glanced at the center table piled high with silver-ribbon-wrapped boxes of spider drones that ranged in size from four inches in diameter to tiny half-inch, eight-legged metal arachnids. Two dozen unboxed drones in different sizes filled out the display, crawling up and down the pile, each wearing a shiny gold bow. "Next year's product is right there. Designed by *me*."

Kevin's ego had always been huge, but this was next level. He thought he could be an absolute prick in front of the company co-owner and she wouldn't fire him.

A chant rose up from the field, and Leah looked at the clock. Five minutes before the show would begin. On the field below, hundreds of drones were laid out in neat lines.

"He's losing it," Nate whispered in her ear, beneath the noise of the crowd.

She nodded. Either Kevin thought he was impervious, or he simply didn't care. It was the latter that terrified her. That was the point at which mass shooters started shooting.

But then, he believed the drones were about to go berserk on the crowd. That her crowning glory would become his crowning revenge.

"I'm going to tell the security guard at the door to keep an eye on him during the show."

"Thank you," she said. There was no way in hell she would miss watching the display, and she wanted Nate to be able to enjoy it too.

She had no doubt now that Kevin had killed Dex and altered the display. He had the skills and the access. He'd likely hoped to blame it on her, say her code failed or she'd sought revenge after being fired, but she had an alibi. A Raptor operator, no less. Pinning it on her would never work. So he'd made Dex's death look like a suicide after he'd uploaded the berserker code.

Kevin expected Dex to bear the blame for the attacking drones.

Everyone at the party moved outside to the stadium seats. Leah and Nate slipped through the exterior door and settled in seats in front of the next box over. She'd gotten what she wanted from Kevin.

Now, it was time to watch the D25DD protocol.

Over the park sound system, the announcer said, "We have an official count of the number of drones on the field, and if they all take flight, we will have a new World Record with one thousand five hundred and seventeen drones!"

"Are people from Guinness here?" Josh asked.

"Yes," Michelle answered.

Leah imagined similar—but much smaller— scenes like this all over the country: kids setting their drones in the middle of the fields in a sea of other drones, then moving to the sidelines to watch the show.

Nate threaded his fingers through hers, and a surprising calm descended. She knew in her soul the show would go off without a hitch.

Tim approached her seat and handed her a champagne flute. He filled it with champagne and then filled his own. He held up the glass and said, "Thank you, Leah. For all your hard work. I know we have you to thank for the show we're about to see."

Behind her, she heard Kevin laugh.

She looked at Tim, a man who'd fired her and lied about it. His comeuppance would come. Right now, she just wanted to enjoy the show. She gave him a stiff smile and clinked her glass to his, and they both drank.

Nate and the others were given champagne, and they all drank another toast as the crowd counted down the last ten seconds to three o'clock as if it were New Year's Eve.

Nate squeezed Leah's hand as first one drone took flight, then another and another. Then four at once, then a dozen. In less than a minute, five hundred drones were in the air, and thirty seconds later, all fifteen hundred were in flight.

Nate's heart pounded as he watched the artistry of the drone dance. The drones were lit with LED lights, and the colors moved but didn't flash. As Leah had described, it was a kaleidoscope, shifting, moving, mirroring. Beautiful and awe inspiring. Four minutes into the show, three new drones joined, and his heart did a little lurch as the dancing drones adjusted to assimilate the newcomers.

For a moment, he'd thought they might go berserk. But they didn't. It was like a ripple in a calm pool. The colors undulated, shifted, and settled back into the new normal, forming spirals and ribbons, gliding through the air the way a figure skater jumped and twirled. At the sixteen-minute mark, more drones joined, and the dance changed again. They formed a row of hearts, the colors lined up so they were rainbows, red in the middle and violet at the outside. Then the hearts wrapped around, forming a ring with the V of each huge heart pointing toward the center.

The hearts separated and flowed into another shape, all fifteen hundred drones forming one giant bird. It opened its wings, and his breath caught as the giant hawk's wings rippled and flapped. Then, somehow, the hawk seemed to soar upward. The hawk dissolved, and now the drones were fireworks arching across the sky, only to come together to form the word "PEACE" in a half dozen languages, before all fifteen hundred drones gently landed in the field below.

The crowd in the stands cheered wildly.

Everyone in the executive seating area was on their feet, laughing, clapping, crying, and hugging.

The twenty-minute-long show had been utterly

exhilarating. Hawk's heart pounded and his eyes were damp. He turned to the woman by his side to see tears streaking down her face. He pulled her to him and kissed her hard and deep. A fierce kiss to show how overcome with emotion he was.

When he finally raised his head, she smiled and had something of a dreamy look on her face. "So, you liked it?"

"My God, that was incredible." He tightened the arm around her waist. "So…the hawk…?"

"It was originally a dove. Last night, I changed it. For you." She rose on her toes and whispered in his ear, "It was the best way I could think of to tell you I'm falling in love with you, Hawk."

He closed his eyes and hugged her tight, absorbing the message he'd felt the moment he saw the giant, beautiful bird in the sky. He kissed her neck, then whispered his reply. "I'm crazy in love with you, Leah Ellis."

He held her, eyes closed, ignoring all the elated people around him. Only one person in this stadium mattered, and she was in his arms.

"I really hate to burst your moment," Josh said, "but Kevin Marks is gone."

Chapter Seventeen

*L*eah paced the room Hawk had commandeered for her once they realized Kevin had slipped out during the show. The same security guard who'd gotten distracted by the display and hadn't seen Kevin leave was now standing sentry outside the door, as Hawk and the others took off to search for Kevin. He was probably long gone, but she understood why Hawk had to try.

Detective Brown would arrive at the stadium any moment. He could have taken Kevin into custody. They'd been so close.

But at the same time, she didn't want to regret watching the show, sharing it with Hawk. The way he'd squeezed her hand and gasped when the hawk formed… She could get high on that moment for the rest of her life without any other drug.

The main suite had been cleared out so Tim

and Michelle could be interviewed separately and together by the half-dozen news crews who were reporting on the event. Tim asked Leah if she could pretend Sunday had never happened and give a sound bite, and she'd done so—she'd be crazy not to take credit when she would probably start her own company soon—then she'd returned to this quiet room with a bottle of champagne and a cheese platter to keep her company.

She messaged Nate to let him know she was back under guard, and decided to pour herself a glass of champagne. After being interviewed by Detective Brown, she and Hawk would go straight to the cabin near Shenandoah. Much as they both wanted Christmas dinner with Freddy and family, as long as Kevin was on the loose, she wouldn't go near the twins.

Kevin must have bolted once he realized the drones wouldn't go berserk. He had to be seething that his revenge had failed.

She glanced at her phone, tempted to read his online posts, but, knowing the words would make her physically ill, she returned the phone to her pocket.

The way he'd killed Dex said something about how much he'd disliked the senior engineer, but there had to be more to it than being angry she'd slept with Dex but not Kevin.

What else about Dex pushed Kevin's buttons?

One thing was certain, Kevin had been thrilled

when she showed up. He'd wanted to see her reaction to the berserker drones. He might have wanted to kill her like he had Dex, but not before she witnessed his revenge.

And now that she'd ruined it?

She felt a chill run up her spine.

Yeah. He'd kill her and probably mutilate her corpse. She was thankful for the guard at the door. They had no way of knowing if Kevin had left the stadium.

A flash of metal on the carpet caught her eye, and she turned to see what it was. A lost earring? She touched her ears. Both studs were in place and there was nothing in the carpet.

She turned, and caught another flash. Bigger this time.

She was losing it. Seeing things that weren't there. She took another step, then saw the spider.

Oh shit. She'd forgotten about Kevin's spider drones.

This one was the size of a half-dollar coin, with a dark matte finish. It was the jewellike eyes that had caught the light and her attention. How did it get in here?

Oh hell. It had probably been on her skirt under her coat. It was small enough to easily hide in the hem or liner.

What could these things do besides listen in? She presumed they had cameras and microphones, and it was obvious they moved fast. She stomped on the drone with her boot, crushing it, then reached into her pocket for her cell phone. She'd call Hawk and give him a warning he was probably bugged too.

She thumbed on the phone then felt a tickling on the back of her hand. Her stomach dropped as she turned the hand clutching the phone and saw another spider, this one smaller than the last. It held on like a real spider, defying gravity.

Before she could shake it off, it leapt to her neck and bit her.

Chapter Eighteen

$\mathcal{N}$ate's stomach took a nosedive when he didn't spot a guard at the door. Where'd the guy go? He shoved open the door to find the room empty and turned to face his boss.

"She wouldn't have left under her own power without texting me." He held up his phone, showing the texts she'd sent when she left to be interviewed and when she'd returned.

Keith cursed. "Marks is still here."

Nate pulled the smashed spider from his pocket. The moment he'd seen it on his sleeve, he'd known what it meant. "And he used one of these to find her."

He scanned the carpet of the empty room and spotted a similar smashed drone. "Leah found one too."

Keith bent down and picked up something from the carpet. He held it out, and Nate saw it was an even smaller drone. It started to move. "Crap! It still works." Then it leapt at Keith's neck. "Ouch! It *bit* me." He pulled it off his neck, and Nate saw two dots of blood, as if the spider was a tiny vampire. "Shit. It probably had some sort of tranquilizer in it. That's how he took Leah."

"It's too small for more than one dose."

"Yeah. That's why I'm still standing. I think I know what happened to the guard."

Nate yanked off his jacket and started patting down his clothes. But if he had one of those on him, Kevin would have initiated it by now.

"They can't have gone far," Keith said.

They'd all donned their Raptor headsets when they went in search of Kevin, and now Keith radioed the others with the news.

All the operatives who lived in the compound had come to the event. Michelle Hollis had kept her word and listed them as hired security, so they had a platoon of armed operatives searching the crowd for Kevin Marks.

Nate and his boss worked as a seamless team as they began clearing offices and suites one by one. They found the security guard one suite over, unconscious, but he roused when Keith checked his vitals.

Nate radioed for medical help, then they left him to continue down the line. The HH party had been held in the Lincoln suites behind home plate, slightly closer to third base. Leah had been left waiting for him in another suite down the row along the first base line.

Kevin couldn't go far carrying an unconscious woman. The man didn't have the build for it, and he'd be noticed if he left the concourse and climbed the bleachers with Leah in his arms.

He must've taken her into another of the Lincoln suites. There were twenty-two to choose from, but Nate guessed the guy would stay on the side between home plate and first base. If he rounded the corner in the other direction, he was more likely to be seen by the press waiting to interview the HH executives.

Movement caught Nate's eye as he scanned the closed suite doors. He came to a stop, holding up his hand to Keith to stop him as well. He pointed down.

There, skittering across the floor, was a tiny metal spider. It slipped under the door to the suite on the end.

Kevin Marks had to be behind the door.

Nate radioed for backup, then they flanked the door. He debated waiting for the others to arrive, but he heard a muffled scream. No way would they wait.

Nate noted the knob was broken—which explained how Kevin had been able to enter the suite, but also meant he couldn't lock the door behind him—and raised a hand to count down from three. On one, Keith kicked the door and Nate entered, gun out, sweeping the room.

The room was empty, but he spotted Leah through the window that overlooked the ball field. She and Kevin were outside, in the suite's reserved outdoor seating section. She had a noose around her neck and was kicking and struggling as Kevin pulled on the other end of the rope, hoisting her up.

Leah's body shielded Kevin. Taking a shot could mean hitting her and risking the bullet going down to the field, where children were lined up, collecting their drones.

He and Keith raced for the exterior door to the outdoor seats. Kevin saw them and hoisted her higher. He'd looped the rope through a gap at the end of a beam, and Leah's feet cleared the seats, dangling in the air. Her free hands grabbed at the rope around her neck as she kicked at Kevin's head and shoulders and missed because he was just out of reach.

Kevin looped the rope around the railing to tie it off. Nate jumped the rail and landed in front of the row of seats below. If the crowd below and behind him saw what was happening on the executive level, he wasn't aware of it, his focus entirely on Leah, who struggled as her face turned deep red.

He jogged over to get a clear shot at Kevin that didn't face the field and fired his pistol right as Kevin dropped the rope without knotting it. Kevin dove for cover, and Nate's bullet hit him in the shoulder as Leah dropped.

She hit the rail and bounced back, bumping Kevin.

Screams reverberated through the stadium as the gunshot registered.

Nate vaulted back over the rail to get to Leah as his boss sprinted past her to chase after Kevin, who'd shoved Leah away, then ran down the row, hopping the rail between sections. He leapt down to the lower level and stumbled.

Nate pulled the noose from Leah's neck. "Can you breathe?" he asked, his heart pounding as she struggled to take in air.

"Yes," she rasped. "A little."

He glanced in Keith's direction and watched as he tackled Kevin, bringing the injured man down easily.

Nate pulled Leah into his arms as he radioed for a medic. "Keith got him, sweetheart."

"One of his damn spiders bit me," she said in a hoarse whisper. "It knocked me out."

"I know."

"I woke as he was dragging me out here to hang me." Her voice was getting stronger already. "I screamed, hoping you'd hear."

"I did." The scream was why they hadn't waited for backup. If they'd hesitated another minute, she'd have been hanging and Kevin long gone before they got to her. His eyes burned as he realized how close he'd come to losing her. And she could have damage to her hyoid or trachea that could still be life-threatening. He pressed his lips to her forehead. "I love you, Leah."

"I love you too, Hawk."

Tears spilled over as he held her and gazed over the park where just thirty minutes ago, a giant hawk had soared above a mesmerized crowd.

Chapter Nineteen

Hours later, there was a knock on Leah's hospital room door. She managed a normal-sounding "Come in," but not at high volume. Her throat hurt too much for that.

The door opened with a drawn-out creak. When no one entered, she said again, "Come in?"

A shiny, metallic drone floated into the room, flying a little shakily, but it was being navigated by camera, so she'd cut the operator some slack. She grinned when she saw the mistletoe hanging from the drone. It flew above her head and stopped, hovering there.

Hawk entered the room and glanced from her to the drone. "Oh look, mistletoe!" He leaned down and kissed her gently, then navigated the drone to park on the chair.

"You're adorable," she whispered.

"Thank you." He took her hand in his. "Word on the streets is they want to keep you overnight."

"Yeah. The doc is ninety percent sure I'm fine given that I never lost consciousness from strangulation, my voice is normal, and I don't show other signs of trauma. I could probably go home, but they don't know what was in the spider bite, so they're going with a better-safe-than-sorry approach." She squeezed his hand. "Don't worry about me, though. I'm fine. You should go have Christmas dinner at your brother's."

"I'm not leaving you in the hospital to have dinner at Freddy's."

"I don't want to make you miss Christmas."

"Sweetheart, I haven't missed Christmas. I got the best gift in the world today." He kissed her hand.

How was it possible that she could be this happy when a few hours ago, one of her coworkers tried to hang her?

But Kevin had failed and would go to prison.

Detective Brown had stopped by earlier and shared what he could of Kevin's motives and actions. He'd written a manifesto of sorts, which had been found in his hotel room. Part of him probably expected to be caught and killed, and his ego couldn't bear not having the world know his greatness.

Much of Leah and Hawk's speculation was correct—he'd hated her for rejecting him, had learned through hacking HR files that Leah had slept with Dex at the previous year's holiday party, and then a week ago, his spider drone had picked up a conversation between Dex and Tim, as they mapped out their scheme to fire Leah and install Dex as the head of engineering.

Tim was trying to seize control of the company from Michelle, and he needed Dex to do it.

Kevin had thought he might finally have his chance with Leah if he was there to pick up the pieces of her broken heart when she was escorted off base. He could even tell her what Tim and Dex were up to and help her get her job back. He drove down to DC ahead of the rest of the HH crew and was looking for a place to pull over near the Navy Yard when Leah was escorted out and got in some other guy's car.

Livid, he followed. Within a few blocks, he realized the driver was taking her for a roundabout ride, fleecing her like a crooked cabdriver. Now he needed to save her from her stupidity in trusting some asshole driver.

Again, he could be her hero, but then in the Mt. Vernon parking lot, he saw her with the driver, and she was all over the guy. And her shirt was unbuttoned.

She was a bitch and a whore, and he tried to run the slut down, but the asshole cheating driver shoved her out of the way.

The manifesto had gone into a long rant about

Leah, which she figured the officer censored for the most part, but the gist was he was mad that an unattractive cougar with no other prospects still didn't give Kevin the time of day. That she'd tried to get him in trouble with HR after she was the one who slept with the office prick who'd stolen Kevin's work and passed it off as his own only inflamed his anger more.

The last part explained the extra hostility Kevin had carried toward Dex. Probably the reason Dex had been stripped before he hanged.

The manifesto had gone on to explain that Kevin had toyed with the idea of screwing with the D25DD code for months and had already written his own version. After leaving her at Mt. Vernon, he made up his mind and went straight to her place so he could get her computer and notebook. He entered the townhouse with a key he'd lifted from the office weeks before. He had his flashlight and would search the office, take what he needed and leave. He hadn't noticed the light on in the back. Hadn't realized Ainsley was there until she called out to him, thinking he was Leah.

When she saw it was him, she'd said, "Kevin, what are you doing here? And why the flashlight? The power works."

He couldn't explain why he was there and couldn't carry out his plan now that Ainsley had seen him. But luck was on his side. This was Ainsley.

He flicked the flashlight switch to strobe and hit her with the bright, flashing beam.

She dropped like a rock. But the seizure wouldn't kill her, and she'd remember seeing him. He had to find a way to make her death look like an accident.

Again, luck was with him. He was truly blessed. A full pan of hot oil bubbled on the stove. The rest was easy. He grabbed Leah's computer and notebook and slipped out the back door before the fire had spread enough to be noticed by the neighbors.

Detective Brown had then said to Leah, *"It's going to take some time to reconstruct the next day as Kevin tracked down Dex and used him to access the Peacemaker servers. But I thought you'd like to know what happened to Ainsley. His version matched your previous statements. Between his writing and your account, a conviction for the murder of Ainsley Weisz is a slam dunk."*

She had more questions but had been given the most important answers for now.

"Where'd you go just now?" Hawk asked.

"Did you talk to Detective Brown?"

He nodded. "Kevin is going to be locked up for a long time. Keith talked to his friend, former Attorney General Curt Dominick. Dominick said what Kevin did to the D25DD code, programming drones to attack over three million—if current estimates on event attendance holds up—Americans, will be prosecuted as an attempted terrorist attack. Children could have died. Survivors would have been traumatized. My guess is the manifesto lays out his brilliant plan because he was so proud of it. You copied his code for the FBI. Several of us witnessed what it could have done. He murdered two people and tried to kill you. He'll go to prison, probably for the rest of his life and then some."

"He's going to claim he's crazy. But he's not crazy."

"He's not, and that defense will fail." He squeezed her hand again.

"I gather he fixated on me because he thought I should be thankful for his attention. I was a desperate cougar in his eyes, and he was angry that even someone as undesirable as me ignored him."

"You are in no way, shape, or form undesirable."

She smiled. "He looked to everything but his own behavior for why he couldn't get laid, and wanted to punish the world for it."

She gazed at Hawk. He'd been celibate for nearly two years but didn't hold others responsible for that fact. The polar opposite of a man like Kevin.

"As his supervisor, I wanted to support him. I hired him. He had a good mind for the work, and I'd hoped he'd become easier to work with as he matured. I tried to mentor him."

"And he probably took that to mean you wanted him, until you shut him down."

"I was oblivious."

"You were a professional, doing your job and expecting the same of the people around you."

There was another knock on the door.

"I think our family has arrived," Hawk said.

Her heart squeezed at the notion of family, and shared, at that. She managed to say, "Come in," but the words came out shallow and breathy. Emotional.

The door opened wide, and her heart grew three sizes at seeing Josh with a menorah, followed by Chase, Tricia, and a few of the other operatives who'd watched the drone show. Each carried a bag of one sort or another.

Josh waved his offering. "I managed to find us an electric menorah. Safe for hospital use."

Tears slipped from her eyes as emotion flooded her.

Chase held up the bag in his hands. "We also heard neither of you would have a decent Christmas dinner, so we thought we'd bring the party to you."

Hawk's hand squeezed hers, and she knew he was overcome with the same emotion. Somehow in this crazy holiday nightmare, they'd gained a big, caring, wonderful family.

Epilogue

Virginia
One Week Later

Leah snuggled against Hawk on the couch in the Shenandoah cabin and watched celebrities she'd never heard of dance on what had to be an icy-cold stage on television. "New Year's Eve is the weirdest holiday, and, arguably, the worst."

"How so?"

"It's this weird buildup to one moment in time that literally is just one second long, then it's over. And for that, you're supposed to get really drunk and make promises about changing your life, when in reality, odds are your taxes just went up and the changes won't last past the second week of January. Also, your car just depreciated."

Hawk laughed. "Well, it's good that you didn't plan a New Year's Eve drone event, then."

"My NYEDD—New Year's Eve Drone Dance—would *kick ass*."

"Agreed."

"It would be so much better than this. I don't know who that singer is, but she's clearly cold and not excited by the idea of her car depreciating. It's messing with her moves."

Hawk laughed harder. "You're right."

"I know I am."

"No, I mean about the fact that you are terrible at watching TV." He took the remote from her hand and turned off the television.

"But how will we know when it's time to count down to midnight?"

"Does it matter? It's only one second in time."

"Good point. But still, I should set my cell phone to tell us ten seconds before." She grabbed her phone from the table and set the alarm.

"I think you secretly love that one second," Hawk said.

"Nah. It's totally overrated."

"We should ring in the New Year by defiling Chase's hot tub while drinking champagne."

"Now that's a celebration I can believe in."

Minutes later, they were both naked in the tub, looking up at a canopy of stars.

"I've been thinking about my New Year's resolutions," Hawk said.

"Yeah?" she asked, her focus on the sky and stars. It was a beautiful, perfect night, after what had been several perfect days and nights in a winter wonderland cabin with the man of her dreams.

"Yeah. Like, I resolve to spend more time with you than I did in the previous three hundred and sixty-five days."

"Well, we've only known each other for the last ten of them."

"Yeah. I've got a lot of making up to do for that."

She laughed. "Okay, I resolve to spend more time with you too." She turned and faced him, knowing where this conversation was going. He deserved her full attention. "Ten days ago, I'd planned to make a New Year's resolution about finding work/life balance. I'd promised myself that I would work less and live more. That I'd spend time with people, not computers. That I'd give relationships a chance. Will you help me keep that resolution?"

"Hell yeah." He kissed her neck, as always being careful of the fading bruises on her throat. "I talked to Keith a few days ago about changing jobs. I don't want to live in the compound. I also need work/life balance, and after eight years of living at the office, I need separation. Keith agreed, and I'm also getting a long-overdue raise. I told him about my frustrations, and he acknowledged he was unconsciously skipping over me with assignments. He's correcting that."

"Hawk, that's wonderful!"

He smiled. "It doesn't hurt that Raptor got great press for our work at Nationals Park."

She ran a hand over his beard. "You deserve every bit of the attention and praise. But why didn't you mention this before?"

"Because I wanted to surprise you on New Year's Eve when I ask you to move in with me."

"Yes!" She kissed him. It was so fast to be taking this step, but it felt so right. She couldn't imagine *not* living with him. "I should warn you, except for the year my mom lived with me, I've lived alone since I was twenty-two. I might be a terrible roommate."

"I can tell it won't be easy by the way you watch TV. I mean, we're all irritated by insurance commercials, but you take it to the next level when you howl like a coyote to block them out."

"Nobody cares about car insurance that much. *Nobody.*"

He laughed. "That's what the Mute button is for. But even knowing how bad you are at watching TV, I can't wait to come home to you every night." He kissed her deeply, then added, "Maybe we'll take up playing board games. Or tennis."

She straddled him. "Or just have sex." She reached between their bodies and stroked his thick shaft.

"We need condoms, which, we've established, don't work great in the tub."

"I have a New Year's gift for you. When I was in the hospital on Christmas, I asked the doctor to give me the three-month birth control shot. Guess how many days it takes to be effective?"

"*Please* say seven."

"Yes! Seven." They'd had the STD talk the day after they first had sex. Birth control was the only reason they'd continued to use condoms.

An alarm sounded through the open door. "Oh! Ten seconds to midnight!" She stroked his erection as they counted down. At the midnight stroke, she slid down on his shaft taking him deep inside her.

He made a sound in the back of his throat and thrust upward. "I don't care what anyone says, that second was totally worth the buildup."

She laughed.

He kissed her neck and said, "Happy New Year, beautiful."

She clenched around him, reveling in the exquisite pleasure of being joined with him. "Happy New Year, Hawk." She kissed him deeply then said, "This might be my new favorite holiday."

Author's Note

In April of 2019, I attended Barbara Vey's Reader Appreciation Weekend and roomed with the brilliant, talented, and wonderful Toni Anderson. After arriving in Milwaukee, Toni needed helium to fill her shark—as one does—and I offered to accompany her to the store. Instead of calling a taxi for us, the hotel gave us the phone number for a car service (I don't have apps on my phone!). En route to the helium store, we asked the driver if he could wait while we bought our shark gas and give us a ride back to the hotel. He told us he couldn't, because he was already booked. Then he added, "These are the worst jobs. My boss always gives me these jobs. A person has been fired and will be escorted from the building by security. My job is to give them a ride home."

Well, you now see what my author brain did with *that*.

Thank you to the kind driver who gave me the plot bunny, and my sympathies to the person who was fired on that April day in Milwaukee.

Thank you for reading *Winter Hawk*. I hope you enjoyed this holiday story!

This is book nine of my Evidence series. The series can be read in any order, and a great place to start is *Incriminating Evidence*, where Nate Sifuentes first appears on scene.

Archaeologist Isabel Dawson finds an unconscious man deep in the Alaskan wilderness, only to discover he's Alec Ravissant, the wealthy CEO and senate candidate she blames for her brother's murder. Now she and the former Army Ranger must work together to find out the truth about his abduction and her brother's death.

If you like steamy military thrillers, check out my Flashpoint Series. In *Tinderbox*, Dr. Morgan Adler has made the archaeological find of a lifetime, which puts her in the crosshairs of a warlord eager to claim Morgan and the fossils. Green Beret Pax Blanchard is assigned to protect the scientist in the scorching desert heat, but can he keep his hands off her when the sun goes down?

Winner of the HOLT Medallion award and named to *Kirkus Reviews*' Best Books.

Visit my website for excerpts & audio samples at www.Rachel-Grant.net

Acknowledgments

This book wouldn't have been possible without plotting help and support from Serena Bell and Gwen Hayes. Both authors also provided beta reads, for which I am eternally grateful.

Thank you also to Gwen Hernandez and Toni Anderson for their valuable feedback after beta reading an early draft.

Thank you to the man who shared his experiences as a driver assigned to pick up and deliver people home after they've been fired, inspiring this story.

Thank you to my children, because you make my world a joyful place. And thank you, as always, to my husband, for continuously showing me what happily ever after means.

About the Author

USA Today bestselling author Rachel Grant also writes thrillers as R.S. Grant. She worked for over a decade as a professional archaeologist and mines her experiences for storylines and settings, which are as diverse as excavating a cemetery underneath an historic art museum in San Francisco, survey and excavation of many prehistoric Native American sites in the Pacific Northwest, researching an historic concrete house in Virginia (inspiration for her debut novel, CONCRETE EVIDENCE), and mapping a seventeenth century Spanish and Dutch fort on the island of Sint Maarten in the Caribbean (which provided inspiration for the island and fort described in CRASH SITE). She lives in the Pacific Northwest with her husband and children.

For more information:
www.Rachel-Grant.net
contact@rachel-grant.net

www.ingramcontent.com/pod-product-compliance
Lightning Source LLC
Chambersburg PA
CBHW061819190726
48289CB00007B/2255